ED

Sallman Ken hadn't been eager for the undercover assignment, but as a scientist he couldn't help being interested in the strange narcotic from the frozen planet—a totally addictive substance unknown to Sarrian science.

It was too late to regret his curiosity now, as the block of frozen sulfur lost its shape . . . its surface puffing into gas and revealing the cylinder containing the alien drug. In seconds it would vaporize. Then Sallman Ken would be a lifelong slave to his craving for it, condemned to serve the outlaw merchant who controlled the supply.

Ken caught the first traces of a sweetish odor, and tried to hold his breath. But he was too late.

The determination to make the effort was his last conscious thought . . .

Iceworld

Hal Clement

A Del Rey Book

BALLANTINE BOOKS ● NEW YORK

A Del Rey Book
Published by Ballantine Books

ISBN 0-345-25805-3

Manufactured in the United States of America

First Ballantine Books Edition: October 1977

Cover art by H. R. Van Dongen

1

Sallman Ken had never been really sure of the wisdom he had shown in acceding to Rade's request. He was no policeman and knew it. He had no particular liking for physical danger. He had always believed, of course, that he could stand his share of discomfort, but the view he was now getting through the *Karella*'s port was making him doubt even that.

Rade had been fair enough, he had to admit. The narcotics chief had told him, apparently, everything he himself knew; enough so that Ken, had he used his imagination sufficiently, might even have foreseen something like *this*.

"There has never been much of it," Rade had said. "We don't even know what the peddlers call it—it's just a 'sniff' to them. It's been around for quite a few years now; we got interested when it first appeared, and then took most of our attention from it when it never seemed to amount to much."

"But what's so dangerous about it, then?" Ken had asked.

"Well, of course any habit-forming drug is dangerous—you could hardly be a teacher of science without knowing that. The special menace of this stuff seems to lie in the fact that it is a gas, and can therefore be administered easily without the victim's consent; and it seems to be so potent that a single dose will insure addiction. You can see what a public danger that could be." Ken had seen, clearly.

"I should say so. I'm surprised we haven't all been overcome already. A generator in a building's ventilation system—on board a ship—anything like that could make hundreds of customers for whoever has the stuff to sell. Why hasn't it spread?" Rade had smiled for the first time.

"There seems to be two reasons for that, also. There are production difficulties, if the very vague stories we hear have anything in them; and the stuff doesn't keep at normal temperature. It has to be held under extreme refrigeration; when exposed to normal conditions it breaks down in a few seconds. I believe that the active principle is actually one of the breakdown products, but no one had obtained a sample to prove it."

"But where do I come in? If you don't have any of it I can't analyze it for you. I probably couldn't anyway—I'm a school teacher, not a professional chemist. What else can I do?"

"It's because you're a teacher—a sort of jack-of-all-trades in scientific matters, without being an expert at any of them—that we think you can help us. I mentioned that there seemed to be production troubles with the drug.

"Certainly the producers would like to increase volume. They would like, of course, to get a first-rate production engineer. You know as well as I that they could never do it; no such person could be involved secretly in such a matter. Every competent engineer is well employed since Velio was discovered, and it would be too easy for us to trace one who was approached for such a purpose.

"You, however, are a comparatively inconspicuous person; you are on vacation, and will be for another year; no one will miss you—we expect these people to think. That's why we took such extreme precautions in arranging this interview."

"But you'll have to publicize me some way, or *they* would never know I existed, either," Ken pointed out.

"That can be done—in fact, has already started. I trust you'll forgive us for that; but the job is important.

The whisper has already started in criminal circles that you are the manufacturer of the bomb that wrecked the Storrn plant. We can give you quite a reputation—"

"Which will prevent my ever getting an honest job again."

"Which will never be heard of by your present employers, or by any respectable person not associated with the police."

Ken was not yet sure why he had accepted. Maybe the occupation of policeman still carried a little subconscious glamour, though certainly it was now mostly laboratory work. This looked like an exception—or did it? He had as Rade expected been hired by an extremely short-spoken individual, who claimed to represent a trading concern. The understanding had been that his knowledge was to be placed at the disposal of his employers. Perhaps they would simply stick him in a lab with the outline of a production problem, and tell him to solve it. In that case, he would be out of a job very quickly, and if he were lucky might be able to offer his apologies to Rade.

For he certainly had learned nothing so far. Even the narcotics man had admitted that his people knew no one at all certainly connected with the ring, and it was very possible that he might be hired by comparatively respectable people—compared, of course, to drug-runners. For all Ken could tell at the moment, that might have happened. He had been shepherded aboard the *Karella* at the North Island spaceport, and for twenty-two days had seen nothing at all.

He knew, of course, that the drug came from off the planet. Rade had become sufficiently specific to admit that the original rush had been checked by examining incoming refrigeration apparatus. He did not know, however, that it came from outside the Sarrian planetary system. Twenty-two days was a long journey—if it had been made in a straight line.

Certainly the world that hung now beyond the port did not look as though it could produce anything. Only a thin crescent of it was visible, for it lay nearly between the ship and a remarkably feeble sun. The dark remainder of the sphere blotted out the Milky Way in a fashion that showed the planet to be airless. It was mountainous, inhospitable, and cold. Ken knew that last fact because of the appearance of the sun. It was dim enough to view directly without protection to the eyes; to Ken's color sense, reddish in shade and shrunken in aspect. No world this far from such a star could be anything but cold.

Of course, Rade's drug needed low temperature—well, if it were made here, Ken was going to resign, regardless. Merely looking at the planet made him shiver.

He wished someone would tell him what was going on. There was a speaker over the door of his room, but so far the only times it had been used was to tell him that there was food outside his room and the door was unlocked for the moment.

For he had not been allowed to leave his room. That suggested illegal proceedings of some sort: unfortunately it did not limit them to the sort he was seeking. With the trading regulations what they were, a mercantile explorer who found an inhabited system more often than not kept the find strictly for his own exploitation. The precaution of concealing its whereabouts from a new employee was natural.

At a venture, he spoke aloud. After all, the fact that they were hanging so long beside this world must mean something.

"Is this where I'm expected to work? You'll pardon my saying that it looks extremely unpleasant." A little to his surprise there was an answer, in a voice different from the one that had announced his meals.

"I agree. I have never landed there myself, but it certainly looks bad. As far as we know at present, your job will not require you to visit that world."

"Just what is my job? Or don't you want to tell me yet?"

"There is no harm in telling you more, anyway, since we have arrived at the proper planetary system." Ken cast an uneasy eye at the feeble sun as he heard these words, but continued to listen without comment.

"You will find the door unlocked. Turn to your right in the corridor outside, and proceed for about forty yards—as far as you can. That will take you to the control room, where I am. It will be more comfortable to talk face to face." The speaker's rumble ceased, and Ken did as he was told. The *Karella* seemed to be a fairly common type of interstellar flyer, somewhere between one hundred fifty and two hundred feet in length, and about one third that diameter. It would be shaped like a cylinder with slightly rounded ends. Plenty of bulk—usable for passengers, cargo, or anything else her owner cared.

The control room contained nothing worthy of comment, except its occupants. One of these was obviously the pilot; he was strapped to his rack in front of the main control panel. The other was floating free in the middle of the room, obviously awaiting Ken's arrival since he had both eyes on the door. He spoke at once, in a voice recognizable as the one which had invited the scientist forward.

"I was a little hesitant about letting you see any of us personally before having your final acceptance of our offer; but I don't see that it can do much harm, after all. I scarcely ever visit Sarr nowadays, and the chance of your encountering me if we fail to reach a final agreement is small."

"Then you are engaged in something illegal?" Ken felt that there could be little harm in mentioning a fact the other's speech had made so obvious. After all, they would not expect him to be stupid.

"Illegal, yes, if the law be interpreted—strictly. I feel, however, and many agree with me, that if someone finds an inhabited planet, investigates it at his own expense, and opens relations with the inhabitants, that he has a moral right to profit from the fact. That, bluntly, is our situation."

Ken's heart sank. It began to look as though he had

stumbled on the very sort of petty violation he had feared, and was not going to be very useful to Rade.

"There is certainly some justice in that viewpoint," he said cautiously. "If that is the case, what can I do for you? I'm certainly no linguist, and know next to nothing of economic theory, if you're hitting trading difficulties."

"We are having difficulties, but not in that way. They stem from the fact that the planet in question is so different from Sarr that personal visits are impossible. We have had the greatest difficulty in establishing contact of a sort with even one group of natives—or perhaps a single individual; we can't tell."

"Can't tell? Can't you send a torpedo down with television apparatus, at least?"

"You'll see." The still nameless individual gave a rather unpleasant smile. "At any rate, we have managed to do a little trading with this native or natives, and found that they have something we can use. We get it, as you can well imagine, in trickles and driblets. Basically, your problem is—how do we get more of it? You can try to figure out some way of landing in person if you like, but I know you're not an engineer. What I thought you could do was get a good enough analysis of the planet's conditions—atmosphere, temperature, light, and so on—so that we could reproduce them in a more convenient location and grow our own product. That way, we wouldn't be forced to pay the price the native asks, too."

"That sounds simple enough. I notice you don't seem to want me to know what the product is—except that it seems to be of vegetable nature—but that doesn't bother me. I had a friend in the perfume business once, and the way he tried to keep secrets in elementary chemistry was a scandal. I'm certainly willing to try— but I warn you I'm not the Galaxy's best chemist by a long shot, and I've brought no apparatus with me, since I didn't know what you wanted me to do. Have you anything here in the ship?"

"Not in the ship. We discovered this place around

twenty years ago, and have built a fairly comfortable base on the innermost planet of this system. It keeps the same hemisphere facing the sun all the time, and we've been able to concentrate enough sunlight in a small valley to make the temperature quite bearable. There's a fairly respectable laboratory and shop there, with a very good mechanic named Feth Allmer; and if you find yourself in need of something we don't have, we can probably afford to get it for you. How does that sound?"

"Very good indeed. I'll take your job, and do what I can." Ken was a little happier at this point, partly because the job seemed interesting in itself and partly because of some of the other's statements. If this product was a plant, as seemed to be the case, there was at least a slight possibility that he was not on a blind run after all. The matter of the need for refrigeration, of course, had not come up specifically—for all that had been said so far, the planet was as likely to be too hot as too cold for comfort; but what he had seen of this system's sun made that seem doubtful. Then there was the reference to warming the *innermost* planet—no, the place was cold. Definitely. Chances improved again. He switched his attention from these thoughts, as he realized that his employer—if this were really the head of the concern—was speaking again.

"I was sure you would. You can give orders for anything you need, starting now. You may use this ship as you please, subject only to Ordon Lee's veto if he considers the vessel in danger." The pilot was indicated by the wave of a supple tentacle as the name was pronounced. "Incidentally, I am Laj Drai. You are working for me, and I am sure we will both be more comfortable if that fact is borne in mind. What do you think should be done first?"

Ken decided to ignore Drai's subtle implication of superiority, and answered the question with another.

"Do you have any samples of the atmosphere or soil of this planet?"

"Of the first, no. We have never been able to keep a

sample; probably we did not collect it properly. One cylinder that was collected leaked and burned in our air, for what that may be worth. We do have bits of soil, but they were all exposed to our own air at one time or another, and may have been changed by that. You will have to decide that for yourself. All that I really know is that their atmosphere has a pressure around two thirds of Sarr-normal, and at its base the temperature is low enough to freeze most of the regular gases out of our own air—I believe it would even freeze potassium. Our mechanic claimed that was what happened to one device that failed to work."

"How about size?"

"Bigger than Sarr—the figures are all at the base on Planet One; it would be easier to look them over there. I don't pretend to remember any of them at all precisely—as a matter of fact, we don't *have* any of them too precisely. You're the scientist, as far as we are concerned; my people are just eyes and tentacles for you.

"We do have remote-controlled torpedoes, as you suggested. It might be well to tell me before you use them; we lost nineteen of the first twenty to reach the planet's surface. We planted a permanent transmitter at the point where the twentieth landed, and we always home down on it now. Just what happened to the others we don't exactly know, though we have a pretty good guess. I'll tell you the whole story at the same time that you look over the other material. Is there anything you'd care to do before we leave the vicinity of the planet and go over to One?"

"Leave the vicinity? I thought you said that world was not the one in question." Ken waved a tentacle at the cratered crescent.

"That one isn't—that's a satellite of Three, the one we're interested in."

A chill came back to Ken's skin. The satellite had been frightening; the planet itself could be little if any warmer since it must be about the same distance from the sun. An atmosphere would help a little, of course; but still—cold enough to freeze potassium, and lead, and tin! He had not given real thought to that. His imagination was good—perhaps a little too good; and it began conjuring up out of nothing in particular an image of a world chilled to the core. It was rough, and an icy blizzard played over it, and nothing moved in the dim reddish light—a planet of death.

But that couldn't be right; there were natives. Ken tried to imagine the sort of life that could exist under such hideous conditions, and failed completely. Maybe Laj Drai was wrong about the temperature; after all, he hadn't been *sure*. It was just a mechanic's opinion.

"Let's see this place, since we're so close to it. I might as well learn the worst," he said at this point in his imagining. Laj Drai gestured to the pilot, and the hull of the *Karella* rotated slowly. The airless satellite slid out of sight, and stars followed it across the field of view. The ship must have spun a full hundred and eighty degrees before Planet Three itself hung in the apparent center of the port. They must be floating directly between planet and satellite, Ken thought. Not wise if the inhabitants had telescopes.

Since the sun was now behind them, the disc of the great world was fully illuminated. Unlike the bare moon, a fuzziness of outline showed that it possessed an extensive atmosphere, though Ken could not imagine what gases might be present. In spite of the definitely reddish sunlight, most of the surface had a decided blue tint. Details were impossible to make out; the atmosphere was extremely hazy. There were definite patches of white, and green, and brown, but there was no way of telling what any of them represented.

And yet, foggy as it was, there was something about the sight of the world which caused the shiver to caress the scientist's skin once more. Perhaps it was the things he had been told, and the things he had deduced from the appearance of the sun; perhaps it was nothing objective at all. Whatever it was, the very sight of the world made him shudder, and he turned away abruptly.

"Let's go to One, and look over that data," he said,

striving to control his voice diaphragm. The pilot obeyed without comment.

Earth, really, is not as bad as all that. Some people are even quite fond of it. Ken, of course, was prejudiced, as anyone is likely to be against a world where water is a liquid—when he has grown up breathing gaseous sulfur and, at rare intervals, drinking molten copper chloride.

2

Roger Wing, for example, would probably have been slightly shocked at Ken's attitude. He was strongly in favor of Earth, at least the rather small portion which he knew. He had some justification, for the country around Lake Pend' Oreille is very much worth knowing, particularly in spring and summer. The first glimpse of the lake each June was something to look forward to; all the way up the highway from Hayden Lake the children maintained shrill rivalry over who would be the first to sight the Ear Drop. Even with only four of them this year, the noise was nearly as great as usual; for the absent Donald had never contributed too much to the racket. Roger, left the senior member by his older brother's absence, was determined to make the most of the opportunity; the more so since it was to last only another forty miles or so. Don was expected to fly to Sandpoint with a friend and meet the family there.

It was, all in all, a hilarious group; and the parents in the front seat had only moderate success in maintaining order. However, the northbound highway from Coeur

d'Alene is a good one, and the disturbance in the rear
was never really dangerous. The principal interruption
occurred when the right rear tire of the station wagon
went flat near Cocolalla. John Wing was a little slow in
stopping the heavily loaded vehicle, and Roger got the
first whiff of the sulfurous odor of burning rubber. He
was to become much more familiar with sulfur during
the course of the summer.

The children were a little quieter after that—the expression on their father's face suggested that his patience might not have much farther to go; but the journey
was never really silent. The causeway across the tip of
Pend' Oreille was greeted with ringing cheers, which
ceased only momentarily while Mr. Wing purchased a
new tire in Sandpoint. Then they proceeded to the small
airport at the edge of the town, and the noise increased
again as the youngsters caught sight of their oldest
brother standing beside a Cub on the grass parking
area.

He was tall, and rather slim, with dark hair and eyes
and a narrow face like his father's. Roger, who had
grown considerably since the last September, discovered
to his chagrin that Donald still overtopped him by half a
head; but he did not let the annoyance lessen the exu-
berance of his greeting. Don shook hands with his father
and Roger, kissed his mother and sisters, and swung
six-year-old Billy to his shoulder. No, the flight from
Missoula had not been eventful. Yes, his final grades
had been good, if not outstanding. No, he had no lug-
gage except the little handbag beside him—a Cub has
sharp load limitations. They might as well continue
their journey, and he could answer questions on the
way. He tossed the bag at Roger and moved toward the
station wagon, Billy still on his shoulder; and with the
crowd settled more or less confortably, they rolled on.

North from Sandpoint; east fork to Kootenai; around
the north end of the question-mark-shaped lake to
Hope, and on to Clark Fork. There the car was left, in
a building that partook of the characteristics of storehouse and garage.

Don and Roger disappeared, and returned with an imposing array of pack and saddle horses. These were accoutered with a speed which suggested the maneuver was not a new one to the family; and the Wings, waving farewell to their acquaintances who had gathered to see them off, headed northward into the woods.

Donald grinned at his father as the town vanished behind them.

"How many campers do you suppose we'll have this year?"

"It's hard to say. Most of the folks who know us have come to mind their own business pretty well, and I didn't notice any strangers in the town; but prospectors seem to turn up when least expected. I don't mind honest prospecting—it lends protective coloration. It's the ones who expect to benefit from our 'strike' that bother me. You boys will have to scout as usual—though I may want Don with me this time. If you've really gotten something out of freshman chemistry, Son, you may be able to help solve a problem or two. If he does go with me, Roger, you'll have a bigger responsibility than usual." The boy nodded, eyes shining.

He had only gradually come to realize the tremendous difference between the way his family and those of his schoolmates spent their summers. At first, the tales of trips to ranches, seashores, and mountains had aroused his envy; then he had begun to boast of his own mountain trips. When he finally realized the atmosphere of secrecy that surrounded certain aspects of those trips, his pride had exceeded his powers of restraint—until he had realized that his schoolmates simply didn't believe that his father had a "secret mine in the mountains." Pique had silenced his boasts for a while and by the time he had developed a convincing argument he had realized that silence might be better for all concerned.

That had been the spring when he was ten years old. His father had somehow heard about the whole story, and seemed pleased for some reason; that summer he had extended to Roger the responsibility which Don had been carrying alone, of scouting the territory around their summer home before and during Mr. Wing's trips into the mountains. The find, their father had told him, was his own secret; and for reasons he would explain later it must be kept that way.

That summer and the two following he had continued to make his trips alone; now it looked as though there might be a change. Don, Roger knew, had been told a little just before leaving for college the preceding fall; his courses had been partly selected on the basis of that information—chemistry, astronomy and mathematics. The first seemed logical, but Roger failed to see the point of the others. Certainly astronomy seemed of doubtful value in anything connected with mining.

Still, he would find that out in due course; perhaps sooner than Don had, since their father seemed to be letting down the bars. His problem for the moment was to figure out a way by which one boy could keep himself informed about every person who came within a mile of the summer house in any direction—and farther than that in some directions. Roger, of course, knew the topography of the neighborhood quite well; but he began right then planning a series of exploration jaunts to make more certain of some points. He was a young man who took things seriously, if they were presented to him in that light.

Like anyone else of his own age, however, he tended even more strongly to fly off on the interests of the moment; and he was easily aroused from his reverie when Edie caught him in the face with a fir cone slyly tossed over her shoulder. She burst into laughter as he looked around fruitlessly for a means of retaliation—there seemed to be no more cones within reach, and the trail at this point was too narrow for the horses to travel side by side. The pack horse the girl was leading formed, for the time being, an impassable barrier.

"Why don't you wake up and join the party?" Edith finally gurgled out between spasms of laughter. "You looked as though you'd just remembered leaving your favorite fishpole in Spokane!" Roger assumed a mantle of superiority.

"Of course, you girls have nothing to do between now and September," he said. "There's a certain amount of men's work to be done, though, and I was deciding how to go about it."

"Men's work?" The girl raised her eyebrows in mock surprise. "I know Dad will be busy, but what's that to you?" She knew perfectly well what Roger's summer duties were, but had reasons of her own for speaking as she did. "Does it take a man to stroll around the house on sentry-go a couple of times a day?" Roger stiffened.

"It takes more than a girl to do a good job of it," he retorted. The words were hardly out when he regretted them; but he had no time to think of a way out of the corner into which he had talked himself.

"Evidence!" Edith responded quietly, and Roger mentally kicked himself. She had been playing for just that. Family rules required that any statement made by a member of the family be backed up with evidence if another member required it—a rule the elder Wing had instituted, with considerable foresight. He was seldom caught by it himself, being a thoughtful man by nature.

"You'll have to let me try, now," Edith remarked, "and you'll have to give me a fair amount of teaching. To be really fair, you'll have to let Margie try, too—" The last was an afterthought, uttered principally for its explosive effect. Roger almost left his saddle, but before he succeeded in expressing himself a thought struck him. After all, why couldn't the girls help? He could show them what he and Don had done in the past, and they might very well have ideas of their own. Roger's masculine pride did not blind him to the fact that girls in general, and his sisters in particular, did have brains. Edie and Marge could both ride, neither was afraid of the woods, and all things considered would probably make extremely useful assistants. Edith was so near to his own age that he could not dismiss her as too young for the work, and even the eight-year-old had at least sense enough to keep quiet when silence was needed and obey orders when argument would be injudicious.

"All right. You can both try it." Roger brought his

cogitation to an end. "Dad won't mind, I guess, and Mother won't care if the work gets done. We'll have a conference tonight."

The conversation shifted to other matters, and the caravan wound on up the river. Two or three hours out of Clark Fork they crossed the stream and headed eastward toward the Montana border; and there were still several hours of daylight remaining when they reached the "summer cottage."

It was hardly a cottage. Built well up on a steep hillside, though still below the timber line, it boasted enough rooms to house the Wing family without any fear whatever of crowding. It possessed a gasoline-powered electric plant, a more or less limited supply of running water piped from a spring farther up the hill, and in general bore witness to Mr. Wing's luck or skill in the prospecting which was supposed to be the source of his income.

A short distance downhill from the dwelling was another building which combined the functions of storehouse and stable. Both structures were solidly built, and had never suffered serious damage from the Northwest winters. The foundation of the house was part of the bedrock core of the mountain, and its walls were well insulated. The family could easily have lived there the year round, and the parents had vague plans of doing so once the children had all finished school.

The first floor consisted of a big room which did duty as dining room and parlor, with a kitchen at one end and bedroom at the other. An open stair well by the kitchen door went down to a basement, containing work benches cluttered with woodworking and radio paraphernalia as well as the wherewithal for various games. The stair to the second floor was at the other end; this was divided into six much smaller rooms, one serving as bedroom for each of the children and the remaining one filled with the various odd articles of furniture and bric-a-brac which are apt to find their way into a spare room over a period of years.

The Wings dismounted by the porch which ran along

the front of the dwelling, and promptly dispersed to their various duties. Mrs. Wing and the girls unlocked the front door and disappeared inside. Billy began unscrewing and removing the shutters on the more accessible windows—those along the porch, and the first-floor ones on the uphill side of the dwelling. Mr. Wing and Donald began unloading the pack animals, while Roger took the other horses down to the stable, unsaddled, and fed them.

By sunset, the house had assumed an inhabited air. Everyone had eaten, dishes had been washed, Billy and Marjorie were in bed, and the remaining members of the family had settled down for a few minutes of relaxation in the main room. There had been some debate as to whether the fireplace should be used, which had been won by the affirmatives—not so much because of the temperature, though even a June night can be chilly in the Cabinets, but simply because they liked to sit around a fire.

The parents were ensconced in their respective seats on each side of the stone fireplace. Donald, Roger and Edith sprawled on rugs between; Roger had just put forth the suggestion that the girls help in the scouting job. His father thought for a minute or two.

"Do you know your way around well enough, in directions other than toward town?" he finally asked Edith.

"Not as well as the boys, I suppose, but they had to learn sometime or other," she countered.

"True enough. I wouldn't want you to turn up missing, and your mother can't be expected to do all the housework herself. Well, Roger seems to have let himself in for proving a point, so let's put it this way. It will be a week or ten days before I go out for the first time. In that time the two of you, working together, will turn in a satisfactory map of the territory within three miles of this house, and a patrol schedule that will permit Edie's housework to be done at times satisfactory to your mother. Margie may go with you, but is not to go beyond the half-mile marks alone—the old rules hold for the younger people, still. That is subject to any addi-

tions or alterations your mother may see fit to make."
He looked across at his wife, with a half smile on his
face. She returned the smile, and nodded.

"That seems all right. Roger has a few duties of his
own, I believe; hadn't they better be included in the last
item?"

"Fair enough. Does that suit you, Rog? Edie? All
right," as the two nodded, "time for bed. You seem to
have the time for the next few days pretty well filled."
The two youngsters grimaced but obeyed; Don and his
parents remained. They talked seriously in low tones far
into the night. The four younger children had been
asleep for several hours when Donald finally climbed
the stairs to his room, but the fact did not lessen his
caution. He had no desire to spend the rest of the night
ducking Roger's questions about what had gone on
downstairs.

In spite of the rather strenuous day just finished, the
entire family was up early the next morning. As a "special favor" to his younger brother, Donald volunteered
to take the surplus horses back to town—they kept only
a few at the summer house, as fodder was a little difficult to obtain. That left the younger boy free, once the
shutters were removed from the upstairs windows, to
get out on the mapping job, as far as his own work was
concerned. Edith was delayed for a while dusting off
china and washing cooking utensils—they had cleaned
only enough for a sketchy meal the night before—but
Roger conquered any slight distaste he might have had
for women's work and helped out. The sun was not yet
very high when they emerged onto the porch, consulted
briefly, and started uphill around the house.

The boy carried a small Scout compass and a steel
tape which had turned up in the basement workshop;
his sister had a paper-covered notebook, a school relic
still possessed of a few blank pages. Between his father's
teaching and a year in a Scout troop, Roger was sure he
could produce a readable map of the stipulated area
with no further equipment. He had not considered at all
carefully the problem of contours.

High as the Wing house was located, there was still a long climb above it; and both youngsters were quite willing to rest by the time they reached the top. They were willing, too, to sit and look at the view around them, though neither was a stranger to it.

The peaks of the Cabinets extended in all directions except the West. The elevation on which they were located was not high enough to permit them to see very far; but bits of Pend' Oreille were visible to the southwest and the easily recognized tip of Snowshoe Peak rose between east and south. Strictly speaking, there was no definite timber line; but most of the peaks managed to thrust bare rock through the soil for at least a few hundred feet. The lower slopes were covered with forest, principally the Douglas fir which is so prevalent in the Pacific Northwest. One or two relatively clear areas, relics of forest fires of the last few years, were visible from the children's point of vantage.

There were a number of points visible within the distance specified by Mr. Wing which looked as though they might serve as reference stations, and presently Roger took out the compass and began taking bearings on as many of these as he could. Edith was already making a free-hand sketch map of their surroundings, and the bearings were entered on this. Distances would come later; Roger knew neither his own altitude nor those of the points he was measuring, and could not have used the information had he possessed it. He knew no trigonometry and had no means of measuring angles of depression.

Details began to crowd the rough chart even before they left the hilltop; and presently the two were completely absorbed in their task. Mrs. Wing was not particularly surprised when they came in late for dinner.

3

The station on Planet One was a decidedly primitive installation, though a good deal of engineering had obviously been needed to make it habitable at all. It was located in the bottom of a deep valley near the center of the planet's sunward hemisphere, where the temperature was normally around four hundred degrees Centigrade. This would still have been cold enough to liquefy the sulfur which formed the principal constituent of the atmosphere Ken's people needed; but the additional hundred degrees had been obtained by terracing the valley walls, cutting the faces of the terraces to the appropriate slope, and plating them with iron. The dark-colored metal dome of the station was, in effect, at the focus of a gigantic concave mirror; and between the angular size of sun and the actual size of the dome, solar libration never moved the focus to a serious extent.

The interstellar flyer settled onto a smooth sheet of bare rock beside the dome. There were no cradling facilities, and Ken had to don vacuum armor to leave the vessel. Several other space-suited figures gathered in the airlock with him, and he suspected that most if not all of the ship's crew were "going ashore" at the same time though, of course, they might not be crew; one operator could handle a vessel of the *Karella*'s class. He wondered whether or not this was considered safe practice on a foreign planet; but a careful look around as he walked the short distance from ship to dome revealed no defensive armament, and suggested that those man-

19

ning the station had no anxiety about attack. If, as had been suggested, the post had been here for twenty years, they probably should know.

The interior of the dome was comfortable enough, though Ken's conductor made constant apology for the lack of facilities. They had a meal for which no apology was required, and Ken was shown private quarters at least as good as were provided by the average Sarrian hotel. Laj Drai took him on a brief tour of the station, and made clear the facilities which the scientist could use in his assigned job.

With his "real" job usually in mind, Ken kept constant watch for any scrap of evidence that might suggest the presence of the narcotic he sought. He was reasonably certain, after the tour, that there was no complex chemical processing plant anywhere around; but if the drug were a natural product, there might not have to be. He could name more than one such substance that was horribly effective in the form in which it was found in nature—a vegetable product some primitive tribes on his own world still used to poison their arrows, for example.

The "trading" equipment, however, proved more promising, as might have been foreseen by anyone who had considered the planet with which the trading was done. There were many remote-control torpedoes, each divided into two main sections. One of these contained the driving and control machinery and was equipped with temperature control apparatus designed to keep it near normal; the other was mostly storage space and refrigeration machinery. Neither section was particularly well insulated, either from the other or the surrounding medium. Ken examined one of the machines minutely for some time, and then began asking questions.

"I don't see any vision transmitter; how do you see to control the thing on the planet's surface?"

"There is none," a technician who had been assisting Drai in the exposition replied. "They all originally had them, of course, but none has survived the trip to Three yet. We took them out, finally—it was too expensive. The optical apparatus has to be exposed to the planet's conditions at least partly, which means we must either run the whole machine at that temperature or have a terrific temperature difference between the optical and electrical elements. We have not been able to devise a system that would stand either situation—something goes completely haywire in the electrical part under those freezing conditions, or else the optical section shatters between the hot and cold sections."

"But how do you see to control?"

"We don't. There is a reflection altimeter installed, and a homing transmitter that was set up long ago on the planet. We simply send the torpedo down, land it, and let the natives come to it."

"And you have never brought any physical samples from the surface of the planet?"

"We can't see to pick up anything. The torpedo doesn't stay airtight at that temperature, so we never get a significant amount of the atmosphere back; and nothing seems to stick to the outer hull. Maybe it lands on a solid metal or rock surface—we wouldn't know."

"Surely you *could* make the thing hold air, even below the freezing point of sulfur?"

"Yes, I guess so. It's never seemed to be worth the trouble. If you want a sample, it would be easier to send a smaller container down, anyway—you can work with it better afterwards."

A thought suddenly struck Ken.

"How about the stuff you get from the natives? Doesn't that give any clue? Could I work with some of it?" Laj Drai cut in at this point.

"You said you were not a specialist. We have tried to get the stuff analyzed by people who were, without success. After all, if it were possible to synthesize the material, do you think we'd be going to all this trouble to trade for it? That's why we want you to get the planetary conditions for us—when you've done that, we'll figure out a means of getting seeds from the natives and growing our own."

"I see," Ken replied. The statement was certainly reasonable enough, and did not necessarily imply anything about the nature of the material they were discussing.

It did not refute anything, either.

Ken thought that one over for a time, letting his eyes wander over the exposed machinery as he did so. He had a few more questions in mind, but he wanted to dodge anything that might be interpreted as unhealthy curiosity, if these people actually were drug-runners.

"What do these natives get from you for this product?" he asked finally. "Is it a manufactured article they can't make, or a substance they don't have? In the latter case, I might be able to draw some conclusions about the planet." Drai sent a ripple down his tentacles, in a gesture equivalent to a human shrug.

"It's material—heavy metals that don't sulfide easily. We've been giving them platinum-group nuggets most of the time—they're easiest to come by; there's an outcropping of the stuff only a short distance from this station, and it's easy to send a man out to blast off a few pieces. I don't know what they use them for—for all I know they may worship the torpedo, and use the nuggets as priests' insignia. I can't say that I care, as long as they keep filling their end of the bargain." Ken made the gesture of agreement, and spoke of something which had caught his attention during the last speech.

"What in the Galaxy is a loudspeaker and microphone doing in that thing? Surely they don't work at the temperatures you mentioned—and you can't be speaking to these natives!"

The technician answered the first question.

"It works, all right. It's a crystal outfit without vacuum tubes, and should work in liquid hydrogen."

Drai supplemented the other answer. "We don't exactly talk to them, but they can apparently hear and produce sounds more or less similar to those of our speech."

"But how could you ever have worked out a common language, or even a code, without visual contact?

Maybe, unless you think it's none of my business and will not be any help in what is, you'd better give me the whole story from the beginning."

"Maybe I had," Laj Drai said slowly, draping his pliant form over a convenient rack. "I have already mentioned that contact was made some twenty years ago—our years, that is; it would be nearer thirty for the natives of Planet Three.

"The *Karella* was simply cruising, without any particular object in view, when her previous owner happened to notice the rather peculiar color of Planet Three. You must have remarked that bluish tint yourself. He put the ship into an orbit at a safe distance beyond the atmosphere, and began sending down torpedoes. He knew better than to go down himself—there was never any doubt about the ghastly temperature conditions of the place.

"Well, he lost five projectiles in a row. Every one lost its vision connection in the upper atmosphere, since no one had bothered to think of the effect of the temperature on hot glass. Being a stubborn character, he sent them on down on long-wave instruments, and every one went out sooner or later; he was never sure even whether they had reached the surface. He had some fair engineers and plenty of torpedoes, though, and kept making changes and sending the results down. It finally became evident that most of them were reaching the surface—and going out of action the instant they did so. Something was either smashing them mechanically or playing the deuce with their electrical components.

"Up to then, the attempts had all been to make the landings on one of the relatively smooth, bluish areas; they seemed the least complicated. However, someone got the idea that this steady loss of machines could not be due to chance; somewhere there was intelligent intervention. To test the idea, a torpedo was sent down with every sort of detecting and protecting device that could be stuffed aboard—including a silver mesh over the entire surface, connected to the generators and capable of blocking any outside frequency which might be employed to interfere with control. A constantly changing control frequency was used from our end. It had automatic heat control—I tell you, it had *everything*. Nothing natural and darned little that was artificial should have been able to interfere with that machine; but it went out like the others, just as the reflection altimeter reported it as almost touching the surface.

"That was enough for the boss. He accepted as a working theory the idea that a race lived on the flatter parts of the planet; a race that did not want visitors. The next torpedo was sent to one of the darker, rougher areas that could be seen from space, the idea being that these beings might avoid such areas. He seems to have been right, for this time the landing was successful. At any rate, the instruments said the machine was down, it proved impossible to drive it lower, and it stayed put with power off.

"That was encouraging, but then no one could think of what to do. We still couldn't see, and were not certain for some time whether or not the microphone was working. It was decided not to use the loudspeaker for a while. There was a faint humming sound being picked up whose intensity varied without apparent system, which we finally decided might be wind rather than electrical trouble, and once or twice some brief, harsh, quite indescribable noises which have not yet been identified; the best guess is that they may have been the voices of living creatures.

"We kept listening for a full rotation of the planet—nearly two of our days—and heard nothing else except a very faint buzzing, equally faint scratching sounds, and an irregular tapping that might or might not have been the footsteps of a hoofed creature on a hard surface. You may listen to the records we made, if you like, but you better have company around when you do. There's something weird and unnerving about those noises out of nothing.

"I forgot to mention that the cargo port of the torpedo had been opened on landing, and microphones and weight detectors set to tell us if anything went in.

Nothing did, however—a little surprising if there were small forms of wild life; the opening would have made a natural-looking shelter for them.

"Nothing even remotely suggestive of intelligence was heard during that rotation; and it was finally decided to use the loudspeaker. Someone worked out a schedule—starting at minimum power, repeating a tape for one rotation of the planet, then repeating with doubled output and so on until we reached the maximum which could be attained with that equipment. The program was followed, except that the boss was getting impatient and arranged to make the step-up each quarter rotation instead of the suggested time. Some humorist recorded a poem on the tape, and we started broadcasting.

"The first result was a complete cessation of the sounds we had tentatively associated with life forms. Presumably they *were* small animals, and were scared away by the noise. The wind, if that's what it was, continued as expected. The first time we increased the noise, after a quarter rotation of the planet, we began to get a faint echo. That suggested that the sound was at least not being muffled very close to the speaker, and if any intelligent beings came within a considerable radius they would hear it.

"To make a long story short, we got a response after the fourth increase of power. We thought it was a distorted echo at first, but it got louder while our power remained constant, and finally we could tell that the sounds were different. They formed a tremendously complex noise pattern, and every one of us who heard them was sure from the beginning that they represented intelligent speech.

"Eventually we began to hear more footstep-sounds between the bursts of alien language, and we cut off our own broadcast. It became evident that the creature was close enough to detect the torpedo by other means than hearing, for the footsteps continued to approach. At first they were interrupted every few seconds by a loud call; but presently the thing must have actually reached the machine, for the sounds suggested that it was walking around at a nearly constant distance, and the calls were replaced by much less powerful but longer and more complex speech-noises. Probably the creatures can see much as we do, though the light is so much weaker on that planet.

"Presently the photocell inside the cargo compartment indicated that something had cut off much of the light. One of the operators moved to close the door, and the boss knocked him clean out of the control room. He took the torpedo controls himself, and began attempting to imitate the voice sounds of the creature we couldn't see. That produced results, all right! If noise means anything, the native got wildly excited for a minute or two; then he buckled down to producing apparently as wide a variety of sounds as his vocal apparatus would permit. Certainly we couldn't imitate them all.

"That lasted for some time, with nobody making any real progress. Nobody had any way of telling what any of the other fellow's noises meant, of course. It began to look as though we'd gone as far as we could, in learning about the planet, and that the knowledge was not going to do anyone any good.

"Then someone remembered the old swap-boxes. I don't know whether you've heard of them; they were used, I guess, before our race ever left the home planet, when people who didn't speak each other's language wanted to trade. They are simply two trays, hinged together, each divided into a number of small compartments. One side is empty, while the compartments of the other are filled with various articles that are for sale. A glass lid covers each of the full compartments, and cannot be removed until something has been placed in the corresponding compartment of the other tray. It takes a pretty stupid savage not to get the idea in fairly short order.

"We didn't have any such gadget, of course, but it was not difficult to rig one up. The trouble was that we could not tell what had been put in the empty tray until the box came back to us. Since we were more interested in talking than trading, that didn't matter too much at the time. We sent the box down in another torpedo, homing it on the location signal of the first and hoping the flatland people wouldn't detect it, opened the thing up, and waited.

"The native promptly investigated; he was apparently intelligent enough to put curiosity ahead of fear, even though he must have seen the second torpedo in flight. He behaved exactly as expected with the box, though of course we couldn't watch him—he put something in every compartment of the empty section, and presumably cleaned out the other; but he put most of the stuff back. One of the things he gave us proved useful—the stuff we still trade for—so we sent the box back with only the compartment corresponding to the one he had put that stuff in full. He got the idea, and we've been on fine terms ever since."

"But about the language?"

"Well, we know his words for 'yes' and 'no,' his names for a few metals, and his name for the stuff he sells us. I can give you either a tape of his pronunciation or a written record, if you want to talk to him."

"Thanks a lot. That makes the whole situation a good deal clearer. I take it you have had no more trouble from these flatlanders?"

"None. We have carefully avoided contacting any other part of the planet. As I said, our interests are now commercial rather than scientific. Still, if you want to send down machines on your own, I suppose we shouldn't interfere with you. Please be careful, though; we'd hate to have contact cut off before we were in a position to do our own producing."

Ken gave the equivalent of a grin. "I notice you are still carefully refraining from telling me what the stuff is. Well, I won't butt in. That's none of my business, and I don't see how knowing it could help me out. Right now, I guess, it would be best for you to give me all the physical data you have on the planet. Then I can make a guess at its atmosphere, and send a torpedo down with equipment to confirm or deny the guess. That will be easier than trying to bring back samples for

analysis, I imagine." Drai pulled himself together from
the rack on which he was sprawled, and gave the equivalent of an affirmative nod. "I'm not saying you
shouldn't know what we get from the planet," he said.
"But I shall most certainly make a hammock from the
skin of the first member of this organization who lets
you find out!" The technician, who had been listening
in the background, turned back to the mechanism of
another torpedo, and spoke for the first time without
looking up.

"That won't be difficult; there's little to tell. The
planet is about three-tenths larger than ours in diameter,
making its volume rather over twice as great as that of
Sarr. Its mass is also over twice ours, though its average
density is a shade less. Surface gravity is one and a
quarter Sarr normal. Mean temperature is a little below
the freezing point of potassium. Atmospheric pressure
uncertain, composition unknown. Period of rotation,
one point eight four Sarr days."

"I see. You could duplicate temperature readily
enough on this planet, by choosing a point far enough
around toward the dark side; and if necessary, there
wouldn't be too much trouble in reproducing the peri-
odicity of night and day. Your problem is atmosphere.
I'll spend some time thinking out ways and means of
getting that, then." Sallman Ken moved slowly away in
the direction of his assigned quarters. His thoughts were
not exclusively occupied with the problem of atmosphere analysis; he was thinking more of a mysterious
race inhabiting the flat, bleak plains of Planet Three and
the possibility of cutting off trade with the planet—
always, of course, assuming that its mysterious product
was what he feared.

He was also wondering if he had overdone his dis-
claimer of interest in the planet's chief export.

4

A circle of three-mile radius has an area of slightly over twenty-eight square miles, or roughly eighteen thousand acres. It follows that the map prepared by Roger and Edith Wing was not as detailed as it might have been. On the other hand, as their father was forced to admit, a tree-covered mountainside does not offer too many details to put on a map; and the effort the children turned in did show every creek and trail of which Mr. Wing had knowledge. Still more to the point, it showed clearly that they had actually travelled over the area in question. This was the defect in the girl's experience which he had wanted corrected before she was released from the "stick-to-the-trail" rule.

He looked up presently from the tattered notebook. The family was gathered around the fireplace again, and the two cartographers were ensconced on either arm of his chair. Don was on the floor between the seats with Billy draped across his neck; Marjorie was in her mother's lap. All were listening for the verdict.

"You seem to have done a pretty good job here," Mr. Wing said at last. "Certainly anyone could find his way around the area with the aid of this map. Edie, how do you think you could do *without* it?"

"All right, Dad, I'm sure," the girl replied in a slightly surprised tone. "Do I have to?" Her father shrugged.

"You know best whether you want to carry this with you all the time. No, you don't have to, as far as I'm concerned. How have the two of you made out on the patrol schedule?" Roger took over the conversation, curling a little closer to his father's shoulder and using the map to illustrate his points.

"There are eight trails leading into the three-mile circle at different points. Don and I used to go around the circle each day, going along each one far enough to be sure no one had been using it. There are spots on each which it's practically impossible to go through without leaving some sort of trail. Going from one trail to another we'd try to cut across places of the same sort—where we could tell if people had been through.

"This time we're working it a little differently. I'm still checking the ends of those trails, but we've been listing places from which people could watch anyone bound away from here—there aren't nearly so many of those. Edie can cover nearly all of them in two hour-and-a-half walks morning and afternoon—we've tried it; and I can do the rest when I take the outer trails. That's a lot like the way you've always worked it when you were going out, anyway; you took a zigzag path, and had us checking for watchers, so that one of us could cut across and warn you if we saw anyone—we never have, that I can remember, but I don't suppose that proves anything." Mr. Wing smiled briefly.

"I may be stretching the precautions a little too far," he said. "Still I have certain reasons for not wanting the place I get the metal to become known. Half a dozen of the reasons are in this room with me. Besides, I think you get fun out of it, and I know it keeps you outdoors where you ought to be this time of year. If two or three more of you grow up to be scientists, we may be able to do some work together that will let us forget about secrecy."

The younger girl, who had been displaying increasing signs of indignation during her brother's talk, cut in the instant she thought her father had finished.

"Daddy, I thought I was supposed to be helping with this. I heard Roger say so yesterday, and you said it the first night."

"Oh? And how did you hear what I said that night? As I recall, the matter was not discussed until after you were in bed. What I said then goes—you can go with either Roger or Edie on their walks, but you still observe the limits when you're by yourself. Billy, you too! There'll be plenty of long trips for all of you, without your having to go off on your own, and there's always been plenty to keep you occupied around here. I've been promising for five or six years to get a load of cement up here if you folks would get enough loose rock together to make a dam out here—I'd like a swimming pool myself. Don doesn't think we need cement for it, but that's something he'll have to prove. I'll be glad if he can do without it, of course." He leaned back and stretched his legs. Billy promptly transferred his perch from Don's shoulders to his father's shins, and put his own oar into the conversation. He wanted one of the trips before his father went prospecting, and expressed himself at considerable length on the subject. Mr. Wing remained noncommittal until the striking of the clock brought relief. He pulled in his legs abruptly, depositing the youngster on the floor.

"Small fry to bed!" he pronounced solemnly.

"Story!" yelled Margie. "You haven't read since we got here!" Her father pursed his lips.

"How long do you suppose it would take them to be ready for bed?" he asked, as though to himself. There was a flurry of departing legs. Mr. Wing turned to the bookcase beside the fireplace, and encountered the grinning face of his second son. "All right, young man, we need some fun—but some of us need discipline, too. Suppose you and Edie save time by popping upstairs and imitating the excellent example of your juniors!" Still chuckling, the two did so.

For some reason, the story lasted until quite late. The beginning was vastly exciting, but the pace calmed down later, and Billy and Margie were both carried up to bed at the end—though they refused to believe the fact in the morning.

Roger tried at breakfast to make the small boy tell

the end of the story and was surprised when Billy refused to accept his inability to do so as evidence that he had been asleep. The older boy gave up at last and went to saddle the horses; he was constitutionally unfitted to hold his own in an argument where the opponent's only words were "I was not either!"

It was shopping day, and Roger's turn to go down to Clark Fork with his mother to obtain the necessities for the next week. They left as soon after breakfast as the animals could be readied. Edie and the younger children went off on their own; as soon as everyone was away from the house Mr. Wing and Don dressed themselves in hiking clothes and headed east. Roger would have given much to see them go.

The trails were good, and for a couple of hours the two made very satisfactory progress. For the most part they followed the creeks, but once or twice the older man led the way over open spurs of rock which involved considerable climbing.

"This is about the quickest way to the transmitter, Don," he said at one point. "It's a lot closer to the house than even your mother realizes—though goodness knows I wouldn't hide it from her if she cared to come on one of these hikes. On the regular trips, I follow a very roundabout path I worked out years ago when I was really afraid of being followed. That was just after the first World War, long before I'd even met your mother. There were a number of people around this part of the country then who would cheerfully have tossed me off a hilltop for a fraction of the value I brought back from the first trip. I tell you, I did some pretty serious thinking on the way in from that trip. You'll see why very shortly."

Don made no immediate answer to this. His attention seemed to be fully taken up with negotiating the slope of loose rock they were traversing at the moment. It was a section practically impossible to cross without leaving prominent traces, and he had been a little puzzled at his father's going this way until he realized that the idea was probably to permit a check on any trailers as they returned. Once across the treacherous stuff and angling back down the slope, he finally spoke.

"You said a while back, Dad, that we were the reasons you didn't make public this source of metal. It seems to me that even that shouldn't have carried weight while the war was on—it might have been better to let the government develop the find and use it. I don't mean that I don't appreciate getting a college education, but—well—" he paused a little uncomfortably.

"You have a point, son, and that was another matter for thought when the war started, with you in high school and Billy just learning to walk. I think I might have done as you suggest, except for the fact that the most probable result of publicity would be to remove the source of metal. Just be patient a little longer—we'll be there in a few minutes, and you will see for yourself."

Donald nodded acceptance of this, and they proceeded in silence for a short time. The course Mr. Wing was following had led them into a narrow gully after crossing the scree; now he turned up this, making his way easily along the bank of the tiny brook which flowed down its center. After some ten minutes' climb the trees began to thin out, and a few more rods found them on practically bare rock. This extended for some distance above them, but the older man seemed to have no desire to get to the top of the hill.

Instead, he turned again, moving quickly across the bare rock as though a path were plainly marked before him; and in a few steps reached the edge of a shallow declivity which appeared to have acted as a catch basin for rocks which had rolled from farther up the hill. Winding his way among these, with Donald close at his heels, he finally stopped and moved to one side, permitting his son to see what lay before them.

It was an almost featureless structure of metal, roughly cubical in shape and a little less than a yard on each edge. There was a small opening on one side, containing a single projection which had the appearance of a toggle switch. Several bolt heads of quite conventional appearance were also visible on different parts of the surface.

After allowing his son to look the object over for a few moments, Mr. Wing took a small screwdriver from his pocket and set to work on the bolts, which seemed very loose. Don, lacking tools, tried a few of the projecting heads with his fingers and had little difficulty with them; in two or three minutes, the older man was able to remove several metal plates and expose the interior of the block to view. Don looked, and whistled.

"What is it, Dad? Not an ordinary radio, certainly!"

"No. It seems to be a radio of some sort, however. I don't know what sort of wave it uses, or its range, or its power source—though I have some ideas about the last two. There's nothing to using it; I imagine the makers wanted that to be easy, and there is only the single control switch. I'm not so sure that the interior was meant to be so accessible."

"But where did it come from? Who made it? How did you get hold of it?"

"That's a rather long story, and happened, as I said, before you were born.

"I was just out of college, and had gotten interested in this part of the country; so I decided to see some of it first hand, and eventually found myself here in the hills. I started at Helena, and went on foot up to Flathead, through Glacier Park, west along the border to the Kootenai, and back along the river past Bonner's Ferry into the Cabinets. It wasn't a very exciting jaunt, but I saw a lot and had a pretty good time.

"I was crossing the brook we just followed up here, just after I had gotten under way one morning, when I heard the weirdest racket from up the hill. I really didn't know too much about the neighborhood, and was a bit on the uneasy side; but I had a rifle, and managed to convince myself that I was out to satisfy my curiosity, so I headed up toward the noise.

"When I got out from among the trees, the noise began to sound more and more like spoken language; so I yelled a few words myself, though I couldn't understand a word of it. There was no answer at first—just this tremendous, roaring voice blatting out the strangely regular sounds. Finally, a little way up the hill from here, on a rather open spot, I saw the source; and at almost the same instant the noise stopped.

"Lying out in the open, where it could be seen from any direction, was a thing that looked like a perfectly good submarine torpedo—everyone was familiar with those at the time, as they played a very prominent part in the first World War. Science-fiction had not come into style then, and Heaven knows I wasn't much of a physical scientist, but even so I found it hard to believe that the thing had been carried there. I examined it as thoroughly as I could, and found a few discrepancies in the torpedo theory.

"In the first place, it had neither propellers nor any type of steering fin. It was about twenty feet long and three in diameter, which was reasonable for a torpedo as far as I knew, but the only break in the surface was a section of the side, near what I supposed to be the front, which was open rather like a bomb bay. I looked in, though I didn't take a chance on sticking an arm or my head inside, and saw a chamber that occupied most of the interior of the nose section. It was empty, except for a noticeable smell of burning sulfur.

"I nearly had a heart attack when the thing began talking again, this time in a much lower tone—at any rate I jumped two feet. Then I cussed it out in every language I knew for startling me so. It took me a minute or two to get command of myself, and then I realized that the sounds it was making were rather clumsy imitations of my own words. To make sure, I tried some others, one word at a time; and most of them were repeated with fair accuracy. Whoever was speaking couldn't pronounce 'P' or 'B,' but got on fairly well with the rest.

"Obviously there was either someone trapped in the rear of the torpedo, or it contained a radio and someone was calling from a distance. I doubted the first, because of the tremendous volume behind the original sounds; and presently there was further evidence.

"I had determined to set up camp right there, early as it was. I was going about the business, saying an occasional word to the torpedo and being boomed at in return, when another of the things appeared overhead. It spoke, rather softly, when it was still some distance up—apparently the controllers didn't want to scare me away! It settled beside the first, trailing a thin cloud of blue smoke which I thought at first must have to do with driving rockets. However, it proved to be leaking around the edges of a door similar to that in the first torpedo, and then a big cloud of it puffed out as the door opened. That made me a little cautious, which was just as well—the metal turned out to be hot enough to feel the radiation five feet away. How much hotter it had been before I can't guess. The sulfur smell was strong for a while after the second torpedo landed, but gradually faded out again.

"I had to wait a while before the thing was cool enough to approach with comfort. When I did, I found that the nose compartment this time was not empty. There was an affair rather like a fishing-box inside, with the compartments of one side full of junk and those on the other empty. I finally took a chance on reaching in for it, once it was cool enough to touch.

"When I got it out in the sunlight, I found that the full compartments were covered with little glassy lids, which were latched shut; and there was a tricky connection between the two sides which made it necessary to put something in an empty compartment and close its lid before you could open the corresponding one on the other side. There were only half a dozen spaces, so I fished out some junk of my own—a wad of paper from my notebook, a chunk of granite, a cigarette, some lichen from the rocks around, and so on—and cleaned out the full compartments. One of the things was a lump of platinum and related metals that must have weighed two pounds.

"Right then I settled down to some serious thinking.

In the first place, the torpedo came from off this planet. The only space ship I'd ever heard of was the projectile in Jules Verne's story, but people of this planet don't send flying torpedoes with no visible means of propulsion carrying nuggets of what I knew even then was a valuable metal; and if they do, they don't call attention to the practice by broadcasting weird languages loudly enough to be heard a mile away.

"Granting that the torpedo came from outer space, its behavior seemed to indicate only one thing—its senders wanted to trade. At any rate, that was the theory I decided to act on. I put all the junk except the platinum nugget back where it came from, and put the box back in the nose of the torpedo. I don't yet know if they could see me or not—I rather doubt it, for a number of reasons—but the door closed almost at once and the thing took off—straight up, out of sight. I was sorry I hadn't had much of value to stuff in my side of the box. I had thought of sending them a rifle cartridge to indicate we had a mechanical industry, but remembered the temperature at which the thing had arrived and decided against it.

"It took two or three hours for the torpedo to make its round trip. I had set up my tent and rounded up some firewood and water by the time it came back, and I found out my guess was right. This time they had put another platinum nugget in one compartment, leaving the others empty; and I was able to remember what I had put in the corresponding space on the previous visit.

"That about tells the story." Mr. Wing grinned at his son. "I've been swapping cigarettes for platinum and iridium nuggets for about thirty years now—and you can see why I wanted you to study some astronomy!" Don whistled gently.

"I guess I do, at that. But you haven't explained this," he indicated the metal cube on which his father was sitting.

"That came down a little later, grappled to a torpedo, and the original one took off immediately afterwards. I have always supposed they use it to find this spot again. We've sort of fallen into a schedule over the years. I'm never here in the winter any more, and they seem to realize that; but from two to three days after I snap this switch off and on a few times, like this," he demonstrated, "the exchequer gets a shot in the arm."

Don frowned thoughtfully, and was silent for a time.

"I still don't see why you keep it a secret," he said at last. "If the affair is really interplanetary, it's tremendously important."

"That's true, of course. However, if these people wanted contact with mankind in general, they could certainly establish it without any difficulty. It has always seemed to me that their maintaining contact in this fashion was evidence that they did not want their presence generally known; so that if experts began taking their transmitter apart, for example, or sending literature and machinery out to them in an effort to show our state of civilization, they would simply leave."

"That seems a little far-fetched."

"Perhaps; but can you offer a better suggestion why they don't land one of these things in a city? They're paying tremendous prices for darned small quantities of tobacco—and a corner drug store could stock them for years at their rate of consumption.

"Don't get me wrong, son; I certainly appreciate the importance of all this, and want very much to find out all I can about these things and their machines; but I want the investigating done by people whom I can trust to be careful not to upset the apple cart. I wish the whole family were seven or eight years older; we'd have a good research team right here. For the moment, though, you and I—principally you—are going to have to do the investigating, while Rog and Edie do the scouting. I expect they'll sneak over to watch us, of course; Roger's curiosity is starting to keep him awake nights, and he has the makings of a man of action. I'm wondering whether we don't find his tracks or Edie's on the way back—he might have persuaded her to go to town for him. There's nothing more to be done here, unless you want to look this communicator over more closely; we might as well head back, and find out how enterprising the younger generation is."

"There's no hurry, Dad. I'd like to look this thing over for a while. It has some of the earmarks of a short wave transmitter, but there are a lot of things I'd like to get straight."

"Me, too. I've learned a good deal about radios in the last twenty years, but it's a bit beyond me. Of course, I've never dared take off more than the outer casing; there are parts too deeply stowed to be visible, which might be highly informative if we could see them."

"Exactly what I was thinking. There should be some way to look into it—we ought to dig up one of those dentist's mirrors."

"You don't catch me sticking anything made of metal into a gadget that almost certainly uses astronomical voltages."

"Well—I suppose not. We could turn it off first, if we were sure which position of that switch were off. We don't really know whether you're calling them with a short transmission when you move it, or whether you're breaking a continuous one. If they use it for homing, it would be the latter; but we can't be sure."

"Even if we were, turning it off wouldn't be enough. Condensers can hold a nasty bite for a long time."

Don admitted the justice of this point, and spent only a few minutes peering through the openings left by the removal of the plates.

"Most of the inside seems to be blocks of bakelite anyway," he said at last. "I suppose they have everything sealed in for permanence. I wonder how they expect to service it? I guess you're right—we may as well go home until the torpedo comes." He slung the pack that had contained their lunch—or rather, the sandwiches they had eaten in route—over his shoulder, and straightened up. His father nodded in agreement, and they began to retrace their steps down the hillside.

Don was wrapped in thought, and his father forbore

to interrupt. He knew how he had reacted to the events he had just described, when he had been very little older than his son was now; also, he had a high opinion of his children's intelligence, and believed firmly in letting them solve problems for themselves as much as was safe. He reflected somewhat ruefully that nothing he could say would be too much help, in any case.

There was no trace of anyone's having followed them at any point on the trail home, though they split up to take opposite sides of the scree they had deliberately crossed on the way out. Neither found this very surprising, for it turned out that Edith had made her scheduled patrols and spent the rest of the day with the younger children, while Roger had gone to town as expected. If he had thought of finding a substitute and following his father, nothing had come of it. Mr. Wing was not sure whether he ought to be pleased or disappointed.

5

Laj Drai found his hired schoolteacher beside one of the torpedoes, checking off its contents with loops of one tentacle. The mechanic was listening as he named off the items.

"Magnesium cell; titanium cell; sodium—oh, hello, Drai. Anything going on?"

"Hard to say. You are setting up a research project, I take it?"

"Just checking some hypotheses. I've listed all the elements that would be gaseous under the conditions of Planet Three, and as many compounds as I could find in the Tables. Some are a little doubtful, since I have no pressure data; they might be liquid. Still, if they are there in any quantity, their vapors should be present.

"Then I eliminated as many as possible on theoretical grounds, since I can't test for everything at once."

"Theoretical grounds?"

"Yes. For example, while fluorine is still gaseous under those conditions, it's much too active to be expected in the free state. The same is true of chlorine—which may be liquid—and oxygen. On the other hand, hydrogen seems very likely, along with hydrogen sulfide and other volatile compounds of both those elements. Nitrogen should be present, and the inert gases—though I don't know how I can test for those.

"I've built little cells containing various materials, along with built-in heaters; and I'm going to warm them up one at a time after landing this torpedo and opening it to the atmosphere. Then I'll bring it back and see what the air did to my samples. I have magnesium and titanium, which should detect the nitrogen, and sodium, and a couple of sulfides which should be reduced if there's much hydrogen, and so on. The report may not be complete, but we should learn something."

"So I should say, from what little I know about it. Were you planning to send the torpedo out right away?"

"Yes; everything seems to be ready, unless there are complications from your department."

"Nothing much. We were just going to send one out ourselves; our native signalled a short time ago."

"Can you control two torpedoes at once?"

"Yes, easily. It occurs to me, however, that it might be best for you to keep a mile or two away from our homing station, and make your descent when that part of the planet is in darkness. The natives are diurnal, we are sure; and it would be a pity to scare them off if any of your chemical reactions are bright or noisy or smelly."

"Or affect some sense we don't know about. All right, you have a good point. Do you want me to wait until you have finished your trading, or go ahead of you if the chance occurs?"

"I don't see that it matters much. I don't remember whether it will be night or day there when the torpedoes arrive overhead; there's a table for figuring it up in the office, and we'll check before arrival time. I'd say if it was day, we'd go right down while you waited, and if it's night you get first shot."

"All right with me."

"You'll have to control from down here—there's only one unit up in the observatory. It won't matter, since you'll be working blind anyway. I'll go up and tell them that you're operating too—we have a relay unit with detection apparatus circling the planet now, and there's no point in having the observers think the flat-landers are out in space."

"Have you been getting activity from them?"

"Not much. Within the last three or four years we have picked up some radiation suspiciously like radar, but it's all been constant frequency so far. We put quarter-wave coatings of plastic with a half-reflecting film of metal on all the torpedoes, and we haven't had any trouble. They only use a dozen different frequencies, and we're set up for all of them—when they change, we simply use another drone. I suppose they'll start using two or more wave lengths in one area or maybe frequency modulation eventually, and we'll have to get a non-reflective coating. That would be simpler anyway—only it's more expensive. I learned that when I had the *Karella* coated. I wonder how we'll get around it if they learn to pick up infra-red? The torps are enough hotter than the planet to show up like novae, when we happen to start them from the ship just outside the atmosphere."

"Let 'em hang in space until they cool off," Ken and the mechanic replied in chorus. "Or send them all from here, as we've been doing," added the latter. Laj Drai left without further remark.

"That fellow needs a whole scientific college," the mechanic remarked as the door closed. "He's so darned suspicious he'll hire only one man at a time, and usually fires them before long."

"Then I'm not the first?"

"You're the first to get this far. There were a couple of others, and he got the idea they were poking into his business, so I never even found out what ideas they had. I'm no scientist, but I'm curious—let's get this iron cigar into space before he changes his mind about letting it go."

Ken gestured agreement, but hung back as the mechanic cut the test controller into the main outside beam circuit—two multiphase signals could be handled as easily as one on the beam, and both torpedoes would be close enough together so that one beam would suffice. The mechanic's information was interesting; it had never occurred to him that others might have preceded him on this job. In a way, that was good—the others had presumably not been narcotics agents, or Rade would have told him. Therefore he had better protective coloration than he had supposed. Drai might even be getting used to having outsiders connected with his project.

But just what did this mechanic know? After all, he had apparently been around for some time, and Drai was certainly not afraid to talk in his presence. Perhaps he might be worked up into a really effective source of information; on the other hand, it might be dangerous to try—quite conceivably one of his minor duties was keeping a watchful eye on Sallman Ken's behavior. He was a rather taciturn individual and Ken had not given him much attention so far.

At the moment he was all technician. He was draped over the rack in front of the control board, his tentacles resting on the various toggles and verniers, and a rising hum indicated that the tubes were warming. After a moment, he twisted a vernier knob slightly, and the torpedo on which Ken had been working lifted gently from the cradle. He spoke without turning his eyes backward:

"If you'll go to the far end of the room, I'll run it

down there and we can test the microphone and speaker. I know you don't plan to use them, but we might as well have them serviceable."

Ken followed the suggestion, testing first the sound apparatus and then the various recorders and other instruments in the cargo chamber which were intended to tell whether or not any violent chemical reactions took place—photocells and pyrometers, and gas pumps connected to sample flasks and precipitators. Everything appeared in working order and was firmly clamped in place.

Assured of this, the operator guided the little vessel to a tunnel-like air lock in one wall of the room, maneuvered it in, pumped back the air, and drove the torpedo out into the vacuum of Mercury's surface. Without further ado he sent it hurtling away from the planet, its control keyed in with a master achronic beam running from the station to the relay unit near Earth. No further attention would be needed until it approached the planet.

The mechanic rose from in front of the panel, and turned to Ken.

"I'm going to sleep for a while," he said. "I'll be back before arrival time. In case you care, you'll be making the first landing. It takes one and a half revolutions of Planet Three, more or less, to get the torpedo there when the planets are in their present relative positions—we can't use overdrive on the drones—and the signal must have come during the local daytime. I'll see you. Have me paged if you want me for anything."

Ken gave the equivalent of an affirmative nod.

"All right—and thanks. Your name is Allmer, isn't it?"

"Right—Feth Allmer." Without further speech the mechanic disappeared through the door, moving with the fluid ease of a person well accustomed to Mercury's feeble gravity, and leaving Sallman Ken in a very thoughtful mood behind him.

Almost unconsciously the investigator settled onto the rack deserted by Allmer, and stared blankly at the

indicators in front of him. One of his troubles, he reflected ruefully, was his tendency to get interested in
two problems at once. In one way, that might be good,
of course; the genuine absorption in the problem of
Planet Three was the best possible guard against suspicion of his other job; but it didn't help him to concentrate on that other. For hours now he had thought of
practically nothing but his test project, until Allmer's
parting remarks had jarred him back to duty.

He had assumed Allmer was a competent technician,
but somehow he had not expected the acuity the elderly
fellow had just displayed. Ken himself had missed the
implication of Drai's statement concerning the habits of
the natives of the third planet; apparently Drai had not
even thought of doing his own reasoning.

But could he be that stupid? He, unlike Ken, knew
the distances involved in a flight to that world, and the
speed of the torpedoes; he had, on his own word, been
trading here for years. What purpose could he have in
trying to appear more stupid than he really was?

One possibility certainly existed. Ken might already
be under suspicion, and facing a conspiracy to make
him betray himself by overconfidence. Still, why in that
case had the mechanic betrayed his own intelligence?
Perhaps he was building himself up as a possible confi-
dant, in case Ken were to grow communicative. If that
were so, Feth was his greatest danger, since he was most
in Ken's company and in best position to serve as a spy.
On the other hand, the fellow might be completely innocent even if the group as a whole were engaged in
smuggling, and his recent words might have been moti-
vated by a sincere desire to be helpful. There seemed no
way of telling at the moment which of these possibilities
was the more likely; Ken gave the problem up for the
moment as insoluble with the data on hand.

The other problem was demanding his attention, anyway. Some of the indicators on the board in front of
him were fluctuating. He had learned the panel fairly
well in the last day or two, and was able to interpret the
readings himself. It seemed, he noted, that pressure and

temperature were both going down in the cargo chamber of the projectile. Well, that was reasonable. There were no heaters working, and the pressure would naturally drop as the gas cooled. Then it occurred to him that the temperature of Planet Three was low enough to freeze sulfur, and his test units would be covered with a crust of the stuff. Something should be done about that.

As a matter of fact, most of the pressure drop was due to leakage; the cargo door had cooled and contracted sufficiently to let air escape slowly around its edges. Ken, however, did not think of that; he found the appropriate switch and tripped it, watching the pressure drop instantly to zero as the door opened. The temperature was almost unaffected—if anything, it dropped more slowly, for the recording pyrometers were now insulated by a vacuum and the expansion of the gaseous sulfur into empty space had had no cooling effect to speak of. A touch on some of the switches which were designed to heat the test substances showed that the little furnaces were still in working order, and after a moment's thought Ken allowed the magnesium and titanium specimens to come up to melting temperature. Then, sure that they were as free of contaminating gases as could be managed, he watched the recorders as the samples cooled again. Through all this, the torpedo hurtled on, unaffected by the extra drain on its power.

For some minutes Ken continued to wait, one eye roving over the dials and the other glancing casually about the great room; but finally he decided that Allmer had picked a good time to go off duty. He did not feel tired himself, but gradually he became convinced that there must be something a little more constructive to do. He suspected that, even if there were to be any drugs around the station, they would not have arrived yet, so there was no use making a search for them; but preparations might be made to see just what came back in the other torpedo.

As a first step, it might be well to go up to the observatory to find out just who was guiding that missile. If it were Drai himself, it would be a point in favor of

Rade; if not, it would be another person from whom information might be obtained. There seemed little doubt that no one would be allowed to run the trading torpedo who did not know exactly what was being obtained on the third planet—the Planet of Ice, as Ken was coming to think of it (not that he thought of ice as a substance; he had never seen the material and would have thought of it as hydrogen oxide in any case. Planet of Solid Sulfur comes closer to the way he would have expressed the thought).

Ken was basing his supposition on his memory of how Drai had refrained from naming the substance obtained from the planet; and, determined to find at least one small brick of data to add to his edifice of information, the investigator headed up the spiral ramp toward the observatory at the station's highest level. No one attempted to stop him on the way, though he met a couple of workers who flipped tentacles in casual recognition. The door of the observatory was not locked, as a trial push showed, and he entered, still without opposition. He was braced for a prompt request to depart, and was a little surprised when nothing at all was said. A moment later, when his eyes had become accustomed to the dimness of the big room, he realized to his chagrin that no one was there.

"No business secrets loose so far," he muttered.

He was about to return the way he had come, when it occurred to him that he might as well make sure of that fact. There were not many places where paper work of any sort could be kept, at least at first glance; and these he rapidly covered. They were mostly cabinets built under instrument panels, and seemed to contain nothing but tables of the motions of the planets of this system. These seemed rather valueless; their most probable use would be in navigation, and Ken could not imagine anyone's wanting to navigate anywhere in this system except to the world of Ice. They could also be used to direct the instruments, if anyone wanted to look at the planets in question; but that seemed even less helpful.

Under the beam setting controls was a small drawer

which also contained two sets of numbers—again, spatial coordinates; but this time Ken froze to attention as he realized that one set at least did not refer to planets—they contained no cyclic term. The set was short, consisting of six groups of numbers containing from six to ten digits each; but he *recognized* them. The first identified by spectrum a beacon star; the next three were direction cosines, giving the three-dimensional bearing to another sun; the fifth gave a distance. Normally he might not have recognized or remembered the lengthy figures; but those were the coordinates of the blazing A-class sun which warmed Sarr, his home planet. The final number was another range; and beyond question it represented the distance from the present point of observation to the listed star. Ken knew enough of the standard navigational notations to be sure of that.

The other set of numbers, then, must give the direction of the same sun relative to some local set of coordinates; and not only was he ignorant of the coordinates, but the numbers were too long to remember. To copy them would be suicide, if anything more than commercial secrecy were involved. For long minutes Sallman Ken stood frozen in thought; then, abruptly, he slipped the sheet back into the drawer, closed the latter, and as quickly as was compatible with caution left the observatory. Since the information was there, it would not do for anyone to get the idea he had been there for any great length of time. It would be better if no one knew he had been there at all, but he had been seen on the way up the ramp. He proceeded to get back to his own quarters and assume an attitude of repose, though his mind still raced furiously.

He knew his distance from home. Evidently the twenty-two days of the journey to this system had not been spent in straight-line flight; the distance was only two hundred twelve parsecs. Score one for Rade; that would be an expensive business precaution, but a normal criminal one.

The direction home *from* this system he did not

know. It did not matter too much anyway; what the Narcotics Bureau would want would be the opposite direction, on Galactic coordinates, and there would be no mathematical connection between the two except a purely arbitrary formula which would be harder to memorize than the direction itself.

Of course, the beacon listed in the stellar coordinates was probably visible from here; but could he recognize it with any certainty without instruments? The instruments were available, of course, but it might not be wise to be caught using them. No, orientation was definitely the last job to be accomplished in his present location.

At any rate, one fact had been learned and one point of probability had been added to the Rade theory. Sallman Ken decided that made a good day's work, and allowed himself to relax on the strength of it.

6

Nearly three of Sarr's thirteen-hour days passed uneventfully before the relay station circling Earth picked up the approaching torpedoes. As Feth Allmer had predicted—and Laj Drai had confirmed, after checking with his tables—the signals from the planted homing unit were coming from the dark side of the planet. Drai phoned down from the observatory to the shop, where Ken and Allmer were engaged in decelerating their missile.

"You may as well drop straight down as soon as you swing around to the dark side," he said. "You will pick up the beacon if you spiral in, keeping between forty and fifty-five degrees above the plane of the planet's orbit, measured from the planet's center. The beam can be picked up by your torpedo more than forty diameters out, so you can't possibly miss it. You'd better ride the beam down automatically until you're into atmosphere, then go manual and move off a couple of miles if you plan to go all the way to the ground. If the natives are camping near the beam transmitter, it would be a pity to touch off your chemicals right in their midst."

"True enough," Ken replied. "Feth is swinging around into the shadow now, still about five diameters out. I wish there were a vision transmitter in that machine. Some time I'm going down close enough to use a telescope, unless someone builds a TV that will stand winter weather."

"You'll get worse than frostbite," Drai responded sincerely. "The time you were really looking at that world, you didn't seem quite so anxious to get close to it."

"I hadn't gotten curious then," responded Ken.

The conversation lapsed for a while, as Feth Allmer slowly spun the verniers controlling the direction of thrust from the torpedo's drivers. The machine was, as Ken had said, cutting around into the shadow of the big planet, still with a relative speed of several miles per second to overcome. Allmer was navigating with the aid of a response-timer and directional loop in the relay station, whose readings were being reproduced on his own board; the torpedo was still too far from Earth for its reflection altimeter to be effective. For some minutes Ken watched silently, interpreting as best he could the motions of the flickering needles and deft tentacles. A grunt of satisfaction from the operator finally told him more clearly than the instruments that the beam had been reached; a snaky arm promptly twisted one of the verniers as far as it would go.

"I don't see why they couldn't power these things for decent acceleration," Feth's voice came in an undertone. "How much do you want to bet that we don't run all the way through the beam before I can match the planet's rotation? With nine-tenths of their space free

for drivers and accumulators, you'd think they could
pile up speed even without overdrive. These cheap—"
his voice trailed off again. Ken made no reply, not being
sure whether one was expected. Anyway, Allmer was
too bright for his utterances to be spontaneous, and any
answer should be carefully considered purely from mo-
tives of caution.

Apparently the mechanic had been unduly pessimistic; for in a matter of minutes he had succeeded in fighting the torpedo into a vertical descent. Even Ken was
able to read this from the indicators; and before long
the reflection altimeter began to register. This device
was effective at a distance equal to Sarr's diameter—a
trifle over six thousand miles—and Ken settled himself
beside the operator as soon as he noted its reaction.
There was not far to go.

His own particular bank of instruments, installed on
a makeshift panel of their own by Allmer, were still
idle. The pressures indicated zero, and the temperatures
were low—even the sodium had frozen, apparently.
There had been little change for many hours—
apparently the whole projectile was nearly in radiative
equilibrium with the distant sun. Ken watched tensely as
the altimeter reading dropped, wondering slightly
whether atmosphere would first make itself apparent
through temperature or pressure readings.

As a matter of fact, he did not find out. Feth reported pressure first, before any of Ken's indicators had
responded; and the investigator remembered that the
door was shut. It had leaked before, of course, but that
had been under a considerably greater pressure differential; apparently the space around the door was fairly
tight, even at the temperature now indicated.

"Open the cargo door, please," Ken responded to the
report. "We might as well find out if anything is going
to react spontaneously."

"Just a minute; I'm still descending pretty fast. If the
air is very dense, I could tear the doors off at this
speed."

"Can't you decelerate faster?"

"Yes, now. Just a moment. I didn't want to take all night on the drop, but there's only about twenty miles to go now. You're the boss from here in." The needle of the altimeter obediently slowed in its march around the dial. Ken began warming up the titanium sample—it had the highest meeting point of all. In addition, he was reasonably sure that there would be free nitrogen in the atmosphere; and at least one of the tests ought to work.

At five miles above the ground, the little furnace was glowing white hot, judging from the amount of light striking the photocell inside the nose compartment. Atmospheric pressure was quite measurable, though far from sufficient from the Sarrian point of view, if the Bourdon gauge could be trusted; and Feth claimed to have worked out a correction table by calibrating several of them on the dark side of Planet One.

"Can you hold it at this height for a while?" Ken asked. "I'm going to let this titanium act up here, if I possibly can. There's atmosphere, and we're high enough not to be visible, I should think." Allmer gestured to the reading of the photocell.

"The door is open, and that furnace is shining pretty brightly. You'd do better to shut the door, only that would keep air pretty well out. A light like that so far from the ground must show for scores of miles."

"I never thought of that." Ken was a trifle startled. He thought for a moment, then, "Well, let's close the door anyway. We have a pressure reading. If that drops, we'll know that some sort of action is taking place."

"True enough." Allmer snapped the toggle closing the door and waited silently while Ken manipulated his controls. Deprived of the opening through which a good deal of heat had been radiating, the compartment temperature began to climb. By rights, the pressure should have done the same; but to Ken's intense satisfaction, it did not—it fell, instead. At his request, the door was opened for an instant and promptly closed again; results were consistent. The pressure popped back to its former value, then fell off once more. Apparently the titanium was combining with some gaseous component of the surrounding atmosphere, though not violently enough for the reaction to be called combustion.

"If you're far enough to one side of the beam, let's go down to the surface," the investigator finally said. "I'd like to find out what percentage of the air will react this way, and for any sort of accuracy I'll need all the atmospheric pressure I can get to start with."

Feth Allmer gave the equivalent of a nod.

"We're a couple of miles to one side," he said. "I can drop straight down whenever you want. Do you want the door open or closed?"

"Closed. I'll let the sample cool a little, so we can get normal pressure after landing without using it all up. Then I'll warm it up again, and see how much of the air in the compartment is used up." Feth gestured agreement, and a faint whistling became audible as the torpedo began to fall without power—like the others, it had speaker and sound pickups, which Allmer had not bothered to remove. Four miles—three—two—one— with deceptive casualness, the mechanic checked the plunge with a reading of one hundred fifty feet on the altimeter, and eased it very cautiously downward. As he did so, he gestured with one tentacle at another dial; and Ken, after a moment, understood. The projectile was already below the level of the homing station.

"I suppose the transmitter is on a mountain, and we're letting down into a valley," Feth elaborated, without taking his eyes from his work.

"Reasonable enough—this was always supposed to be a rough section of the planet," agreed Ken. "It's good—there's that much less chance of being visible from a distance. What's the matter—aren't you down, after all?"

The altimeter had reached zero, but nothing had checked the descent. Faint rustlings had become audible in the last few seconds, and now these were supplemented by louder snappings and cracklings. Descent ceased for a moment. Apparently an obstacle sufficient to reflect radar waves and take the machine's weight had been encountered; but when a little downward drive was applied, the crackling progress continued for some distance. Finally, however, it ceased—noise and motion alike—even when Allmer doubled and quadrupled the power for several seconds. He opened his drive switches and turned to Ken with a gesture equivalent to a shrug.

"We seem to be down, though I can't guarantee it's ground as we know it. It seems to be as low as we can get, though. There's the door switch, in case you didn't know. You're on your own, unless you don't mind my hanging around to watch. I suppose the boss will be here soon, too; he should have his machine in an orbit by this time."

"Sure—stick around. I'll be glad to have you. Maybe we'll have to move the thing around, for all I can tell at the moment." He had opened the door as he spoke, and watched with interest as the pressure gauge snapped up to a value about two thirds of Sarr normal. At the same instant, the temperature dial of the still hot titanium furnace began to rise spontaneously—apparently the greater atmospheric density was more than able to offset the slight amount of cooling that had taken place; the metal was actually burning. Ken hastily shut the door.

The temperature continued to rise a short distance, while the light intensity in the cargo compartment of the torpedo held at a value that would have been intense even to eyes accustomed to Sarr's fervent sun. The most interesting information, however, came from the pressure gauge; and it was on this that Ken kept his attention glued.

For perhaps twenty seconds the reaction continued unabated; then it began to die out, and in ten more the temperature began once more to drop. The reason was evident; pressure had dropped to less than two percent of its former value. There was literally nothing left to carry on the reaction.

Ken emitted the booming drone from his sound-diaphragm that was the Sarrian equivalent of a whistle of surprise.

"I knew molten titanium would react to completion in our atmosphere, but I didn't think it would possibly do it here. I guess I was wrong—I was rather expecting a mixture of compounds, whose heats of formation would prevent any such reaction. Still, I suppose at this planet's temperature, they wouldn't have to be very stable from our point of view . . ." his voice trailed off.

"Means nothing to me, but it certainly burned," Feth Allmer remarked. "How about your other samples? Are you going to run them off right away, or wait for things to cool down again to planet-normal?" Another dial caught Ken's eye before he could answer.

"Hey—who lit the sodium?" he asked, heedless of Allmer's query. "It's cooling now, but it must have been burning, too, for a while when there was air."

"Let more in and see." The toggle snapped over, and there was a distinct popping sound as air rushed into the rear-vacuum. The sodium continued to cool.

"Maybe a spark from the titanium pot lighted it up." Without answering, Ken closed the door once more and began to warm up the sodium container. Apparently Feth's suggestion was not too far from the mark; very little additional heat was needed to ignite the metal. This time the reaction stopped after pressure had dropped about a sixth. Then the door was opened again, and another touch of artificial heat caused the reaction to resume. This time it continued, presumably, until the sodium was consumed.

"I want enough material to work on when we get it back," Ken explained, "I'm not the Galaxy's best analytical chemist."

The crucible of carbon dust gave decidedly peculiar results. *Something* certainly happened, for the material not only maintained but even increased its temperature for some time after the heating current was cut off; but there was no evidence either of consumption or production of gas in the closed chamber. Both Ken and Feth were slightly startled. The former, in response to the mechanic's quizzical expression, admitted the fact was probably significant but could offer no explanation.

Samples of iron, tin, lead, and gold followed in due course. None of these seemed greatly affected by the peculiar atmosphere at any temperature, with the possible exception of the iron; there the pressure drop was too small to be certain, since in each of these cases the heating had caused an increase in pressure which had to be allowed for. Magnesium behaved remarkably like sodium, except that it burned even more brightly than the titanium.

Here again Ken decided to finish off the metal by relighting it with the door open; and here the testing program received a sudden interruption.

Both Sarrians were perfectly aware that with the door open a beam of light must be stabbing out into the darkness. Both had ceased to worry about the fact; it had been equally true, though perhaps the radiance was fainter, with the blazing sodium and almost as much so when the sheer heat of the samples of iron and gold had been exposed. They had completely ceased to worry about being seen; a full hour had already passed since they had landed the torpedo, owing to the cooling periods necessary between tests, and there had been no sign that any attention had been attracted. Ken should have remembered the difficulty that had been encountered in reaching the ground.

The possibility was brought back to their attention with the relighting of the magnesium sample. As the photocell reported the reestablishment of combustion, a shrill sound erupted from the speaker above the control board and echoed through the ship. Neither had to be told what it was; both had heard the recordings of the voice of the Third Planet native who had found the original torpedo.

For an instant both remained frozen on their racks, exploring mentally the possibilities of the situation. Feth made a tentative gesture toward the power switches, only to be checked by an imperious snap of Ken's tentacles.

"Wait! Is our speaker on?" The words were whispered.

"Yes." Feth pulled a microphone down to chest level and retreated a step. He wanted no part in what Ken seemed about to do. Sallman himself, however, had once more become completely absorbed in the mystery of the World of Ice, to the exclusion of all other matters; he saw no reason for leaving the site where his activities had been discovered. It did not even occur to him not to answer the native who appeared to have made the discovery. With his speaking diaphragm close to the microphone, he emulated the "boss" of so many years before, and tried to imitate the sounds coming from the speaker.

The result was utter silence.

At first neither listener worried; the native would naturally be surprised. Gradually, however, an expression of mild anxiety began to appear on Ken's features, while an "I-told-you-so" air became manifest about Feth.

"You've scared him away," the latter finally said. "If his tribe stampedes with him, Drai won't be very happy about it."

A faint crackling which had preceded the alien's call, and which his concentration of chemical problems had prevented reaching Ken's conscious mind, suddenly ballooned into recollection, and he snatched at the straw.

"But we heard him coming—the same sort of noise the torpedo made landing—and we haven't heard him leave. He must still be waiting."

"Heard him coming? Oh—that? How do you know that's what it was? Neither of us was paying any attention."

"What else could it have been?" This was a decidedly unfair question, to which Feth attempted no direct answer. He simply countered with another.

"What's he waiting for, then?" Fate was unkind to him; Ken was spared the necessity of answering. The human voice came again, less shrill this time; history seemed to be repeating itself. Ken listened intently; Feth seemed to have forgotten his intention of dissociating himself from the proceedings and was crowded as close as the detective to the speaker. The voice went on, in short bursts which required little imagination to interpret as questions. Not a word was understandable, though both thought they recognized the human "no" on several occasions. Certainly the creature did not utter any of the names that the Sarrians had come to associate with trade items—Feth, who knew them all, was writing them on a scrap of paper. Ken finally grew impatient, took the list from the mechanic, and began to pronounce them as well as he could, pausing after each.

"Iridium—Flatinum—Gold—Osmium—"

"Gold!" the unseen speaker cut in.

"Gold!" responded Ken intelligently, into the microphone, and "which one is that?" in a hasty aside to Feth. The mechanic told him, also in a whisper. "There's a sample in the torpedo. We can't trade it off—I want to analyze it for traces of corrosion. Anyway it was melted a little while ago, and he'll never get it out of the crucible. What's the name for the stuff you get from them?"

"Tofacco." Feth answered without thinking—but he started thinking immediately afterward. He remembered Drai's promise of the fate of anyone who gave Ken information about "the stuff" obtained from Earth, and knew rather better than Sallman just how jocular Laj was likely to be. The memory made him itch, as though his hide were already coming loose. He wondered how he could keep news of his slip from reaching the higher levels, but had no time to get a really constructive idea. The speaker interrupted him again.

If the previous calls had been loud, this was explosive. The creature must have had his vocal apparatus within inches of the torpedo's microphone, and been using full voice power to boot. The roar echoed for seconds through the shop and almost drowned out the clanking which followed—a sound which suggested something hard striking the hull of the torpedo. The native, for some reason, seemed to have become wildly excited.

At almost the same instant, Ken also gave an exclamation. The thermometer dial for the gold sample had ceased to register.

"The blasted savage is stealing my sample!" he howled, and snapped over the switch closing the cargo door. The switch moved, but the door apparently didn't—at least, it failed to indicate "locked." There was no way of telling whether or not it had stopped at some partly-closed position.

The native was still jabbering—more than ever, if that were possible. Ken switched back to "open" position, waited a moment, and tried to close again. This time it worked. The Sarrians wondered whether the relatively feeble motor which closed the portal had been able to cause any injury. There seemed little doubt about the cause of the first failure; if there had been any, the noise would have removed it.

"I don't think he was trying to steal," Feth said mildly. "After all, you repeated the name of the stuff more than once. He probably thought you were offering it to him."

"I suppose you may be right." Ken turned back to the microphone. "I'll try to make clear that it's market day, not a wedding feast." He gave a chirruping whistle, then "Tofacco! tofacco! Gold—tofacco!" Feth shrivelled, internally. If he could only learn to keep his big diaphragm frozen—.

"Tofacco! Gold—tofacco! I wonder whether that will mean anything to him?" Ken turned a little away from the microphone. "This may not be one of the creatures you've been trading with—after all, we're not in the usual place."

"That's not the principal question!" Feth's tentacles coiled tightly around his torso, as though he were expecting a thunderbolt to strike somewhere in the neighborhood. The voice which had made the last statement was that of Laj Drai.

7

Roger Wing, at thirteen years of age, was far from stupid. He had very little doubt where his father and brother had been, and he found the fact of considerable interest. A few minutes' talk with Edie gave him a fairly accurate idea of how long they had been gone; and within ten minutes of the time he and his mother returned from Clark Fork he had sharply modified his older ideas about the location of the "secret mine." Hitherto, his father had always been away several days on his visits to it.

"You know, Edie, that mine can't be more than eight or ten miles from here, at the outside." The two were feeding the horses, and Roger had made sure the younger children were occupied elsewhere. "I talked to Don for about two minutes, and I know darned well Dad was showing him the mine. I'm going to see it, too, before the summer's out. I'll take bets on it."

"Do you think you ought to? After all, if Dad wanted us to know, he'd tell us."

"I don't care. I have a right to know anything I can find out. Besides, we can do a better job of scouting if we know the place we're supposed to be protecting."

"Well—maybe."

"Besides, you know Dad sometimes sets things up just so we'll find things out for ourselves. After it's all over he just says that's what we have brains for. Remember he never actually *said* we weren't to go looking for the mine—he just said he'd tell us when the time came. How about that?"

"Well—maybe. What are you going to do about it? If you try to follow Dad you'll be picked up like a dime in a schoolroom."

"That's what you think. Anyway, I'm not going to follow him. I'll lead him. I'll go out the first thing to-morrow morning and look for any traces they may have left. Then the next time they go, I'll be waiting for them at the farthest trace I could find, and go on from there. That'll work, for sure!"

"Who does the patrolling?"

"Oh, we both do, same as before. This won't take long. Anyway, like I said, since I'll be watching the trail they take, it'll be even better than the regular patrol. Don't you think?" Edie looked a little dubious as she latched the door of the feed bin.

"You'll probably get away with it, but I bet you'll have to talk fast," was her verdict as they headed for the house.

Twenty-four hours later Roger was wondering whether any excuses would be needed at all. Things had not gone according to his sweepingly simple forecast.

In the first place, he had not had time to check any trail his father and Don might have left; for the two started out at daybreak the next morning. They did not follow the previous day's route, but the one Mr. Wing had always taken in years past—the admittedly zigzag path specifically designed to permit his scouts to take short cuts to warn him, in the event that anyone followed. Roger and Edith were given stations which were to be watched for one hour after the two men had passed; each was then to intercept the trail and make a report, whether or not anyone had been seen. Roger looked suspiciously at his sister for an instant when those orders were received, but decided she would never have told his plans. His father was simply one jump ahead, as usual.

A good fraction of the morning had passed by the time he had made his report, and watched his father and brother disappear to the north. This was not the direction they had gone the day before, according to Edith; now the question was whether or not they had bothered to lay a false trail on that occasion, too. The only way to settle that appeared to be a straightforward search for traces. That was not too hopeless; as Roger had said while telling his father about the new patrol arrangements, there were places practically impossible to cross without leaving some sort of track, and the mere act of avoiding all those places would narrow down considerably the routes a person could take.

In spite of this, the boy had decided by dinner time that either he knew less about tracking than he had supposed or else the two he sought had spent the day in the attic. Certainly he had found nothing to which he could point with confidence as being evidence of their passage.

After the meal he had abandoned that line of research, and simply headed eastward. His sister had said they had taken this direction, and there was the remote chance that they might have abandoned precautions just that once. He travelled without pause for nearly half the afternoon, following what seemed to be natural trails, and finally stopped some eight miles from home.

He found himself in a valley, its center marked as usual by a noisy brook. The hills on either side were high, though by no means as high as some of their neighbors—six to seven thousand feet was a common height in this part of the range. He had not been here before, either alone or with his father, but still felt he had a good idea of his location. His principal worry was the fact that he had as yet seen no sign of his father or brother.

His intention was to work back toward the house from this point, zigzagging to cover as much territory as possible before dark. The first zig, he decided, should take him straight up the side of the hill to the south, thus crossing any possible trails cutting around this side of the mountain. After reaching the top, he could decide whether to go down the other side at once, or head west a short distance before sweeping back to the north. As it turned out, he never had to make that decision.

Roger Wing was not, of course, as competent a tracker as he liked to believe. As a matter of fact, he had crossed the trail he was so diligently seeking four times since leaving the house. His present location was at the foot of the hill bearing the open slope which the "miners" had crossed the day before, and within a mile of the Sarrian homing station. The course he now took uphill would have led him within a few rods of the transmitter.

However, he didn't get that far. Donald had been perfectly correct in concluding that no one could cross that slope of loose rock without leaving traces. Roger failed to recognize the marks left by the two on the way out, but he did find where his brother had forced his way through an unusually thick patch of brush at the top of the scree on the way back. It was carelessness on the older boy's part, of course; his attention at the time had been mainly taken up with the search for tracks left by the possible followers, and he had paid no attention to those he himself was leaving. While the broken bushes gave Roger no clue to the traveller's identity, they indicated his direction very clearly; and the boy promptly turned westward. Had he stopped to think, it would have occurred to him that a trail in this direction hardly jibed with the assumption that his father and brother were going straight to the "mine"; but he was not thinking at the moment. He was tracking, as he would have told anyone who might have asked.

Once out of the patch of brush, the trail was neither more nor less obvious than it had been all along; but Roger was able to follow it. Probably the assurance that there was a trail to follow had something to do with that. He still did not know whether the traces had been left by his father, his brother, or both. He also failed to recognize the point where the two had come together after covering both sides of the scree. He simply went on, picking out the occasional scuff in the carpet of fir needles or snapped twigs where the bushes were thicker.

He descended the west side of the hill, after following it around from the point where the first traces had appeared. He crossed the narrow valley on this side, leaping the inevitable brook with little difficulty. Here he found the only assurance that he was actually following two people, in the indentations where they had landed on the bank after a similar leap. The marks were just dents, for the needles did not retain any definite shoe patterns, but there were four of them. They were in two pairs, one of each deeper than its fellow, as though the jumper had taken the shock of landing principally on one foot.

Up the side of the next hill the boy went. It was darker now under the trees, for the sun was already concealed by the peak ahead of him; and presently he began to wonder whether he were really on the right trail. He stopped, looking about, and saw first to one side and then the other marks of the sort he had been following. He could not, he found, convince himself that those ahead of him were the right ones.

He tried to go on, then hesitated again. Then he began to backtrack—and reached the brook many yards from the spot at which he had jumped it. He spent some minutes searching for the marks, and when he had found them realized that he had not even followed his own back trail with any accuracy.

He should, of course, have headed for home right then. Equally, of course, he did nothing of the sort. While the gloom on the mountain's eastward face grew ever deeper, he cast about for tracks. Every few minutes he found something, and spent long seconds over it before deciding to make sure—and then he always found something else. Gradually he worked his way up the mountain side, finally reaching open rock; and after deep thought, he moved around to the other side where it was lighter, and resumed his search. After all, the men had been heading westward.

He had crossed another valley—this time its central watercourse was dry, and there was no sign of anyone's jumping over—and was near the top of the unusually low hill on its farther side when he finally realized the time. He had been searching with a single-mindedness which had prevented even hunger from forcing itself on his attention. The sheer impossibility of seeing details on the shadowed ground was all that finally compelled him to consider other matters. He had no flashlight, as he had not contemplated remaining out this late. Worse, he had neither food, water, nor a blanket. The first two were serious omissions, or would be if his father heard of his venturing any distance into the woods without them.

It was quite suddenly borne in upon Roger Wing, as he saw the first stars glimmering in the deepening blue between the tree tops, that he was not another Daniel Boone or Kit Carson. He was a thirteen year old boy whose carelessness had gotten him into a situation that was certainly going to be uncomfortable and might even be serious.

Though rash, Roger was not stupid. His first action upon realizing the situation was not a wild break for home. Instead he sensibly stood where he was and proceeded to plan a course of action.

He was certainly going to be cold that night. There was no help for that, though a shelter of fir branches would make some difference. Also, there was no food, or at least none that he would be able to find in the dark. Water, however, should be findable; and, after all, it was the greatest necessity. Remembering that the valley he had just crossed lacked a stream, the boy started on again over the low top in front of him and began to pick his way down the other side. He was forced to rely almost entirely on touch before he reached the bottom, for the lingering twilight made little impression on the gloom beneath the firs. He found a brook, as he had hoped, partly by sound and partly by almost falling over the bank.

He did have a knife, and with this he cut enough fir branches to make a bed near the stream, and to lean against a fallen log beside it as a crude roof—he knew that anything at all to break air circulation immediately

over his body would be a help. He then drank, loosened
his belt, and crawled under the rude shelter. All things
considered, he was not too long in going to sleep.

He was a healthy youngster, and the night was not
particularly cold. He slept soundly enough so that the
crackling and crashing of branches in the forest roof
failed to awaken him, and even the louder crunching as
Ken's torpedo settled through the underbrush forty
yards away only caused him to mutter sleepily and turn
over.

But he was awakened at last, by the stimulus which
sends any forest resident into furious activity. The cargo
door of the torpedo faced the boy's shelter. The light
from burning sodium and glowing gold and iron did not
disturb him—perhaps they only gave him bad dreams,
or perhaps he was facing the other way at the time. The
blazing radiance of the burning magnesium, however,
blasted directly onto his closed eyelids, and enough of it
got through to ring an alarm. He was on his feet yelling
"Fire," before he was fully awake.

He had seen the aftermath of more than one forest
fire—there had been a seventy-five hundred acre blaze
the summer before north of Bonner's Ferry, and a
smaller but much closer one near Troy. He knew what
such a catastrophe meant for life in its path, and for
several seconds was completely panic-stricken. He even
made a leap away from the direction of the radiance,
and was brought to his senses by the shock of falling
over the tree trunk beside which he had been sleeping.

Coming to his feet more slowly, he realized that the
light was not the flickering, ruddy glow of wood flames,
that there was none of the crackling roar he had heard
described more than once, and that there was no smell
of smoke. He had never seen magnesium burn, but the
mere fact that this was not an ordinary forest fire allowed his curiosity to come once more into the fore-
ground.

The light was sufficient to permit him to clear the
little stream without difficulty, and in a matter of seconds he had crashed through the underbrush to its

source, calling as he went, "Hello! Who's that? What's that light?"

The booming grumble of Sallman Ken's answer startled him out of his wits. The drumlike speaking diaphragm on the Sarrian torso can be made to imitate most human speech sounds, but there is a distortion that is readily apparent to any human ear; and the attempt to imitate his words in those weird tones sent prickling chills down the boy's spine. The fact that he *could* recognize his own words in the booming utterance made it, if anything, rather worse.

He stopped two yards from the torpedo, wondering. The blue-white glare from the rectangular opening had died away abruptly as he approached, and had been replaced by a fading yellow-white glow as the crucible which had contained the magnesium slowly cooled. He could just see into the door. The chamber beyond seemed to occupy most of the interior of that end of the structure, as nearly as he could tell from his inadequate view of the outside, and its door was covered with roughly cylindrical objects a trifle larger than his fist. One of these was the source of the white-hot glow, and at least two others still radiated a dull red. He had noticed only this much when Ken began to go through his precious-metals list.

Roger knew, of course, what platinum and iridium were, even when the former suffered from the peculiarities of the Sarrian vocal apparatus; but like many other human beings, it was the mention of gold that really excited him. He repeated the word instantly.

"Gold!"

"Gold." The booming voice from the torpedo responded, and Roger found the courage to approach the still radiant doorway, and look in. As he had guessed, the little cylindrical crucibles were everywhere. The chamber was covered with white dust, the oxides of titanium and magnesium which had sprayed from the containers during the energetic reactions which had produced them. Tiny yellowish globules of sodium peroxide were spread almost as widely. A noticeable wave of heat could still be felt coming from the chamber along with a faint sulfurous smell, but when Roger laid a cautious hand in the dust of its floor the temperature proved to be bearable. He saw almost instantly what he supposed the hidden speaker had been talking about—the gold which had already solidified in its small container. The light was bright enough for him to recognize it, particularly since there was nothing else of even approximately the same color in the chamber.

The box acted instantly, but with more forethought than might have been expected. A dead branch which he picked up as he approached was put to use—the door of the compartment reminded him too much of a trap, and he propped it open. Then he made a grab for the pot of gold.

He did not see the wires which connected its heater to the power source of the torpedo. After touching the crucible, he did not even look for them, though they were the only reason he did not succeed in getting the container out. He had time for one good tug before the fact that the metal had only recently been melted made itself felt.

Roger, his face almost inside the compartment, yelled even more whole-heartedly then he had before, released the crucible, delivered a furious kick on the hull of the torpedo, and danced about, holding his scorched hand and hurling abuse at the unseen beings who had been responsible for the injury. He did not notice the stick which he had used as a prop suddenly snap as the door started to close, or the thud as the portal jammed against the fragments of wood. The sudden cutting off of nearly all the light, however, did catch his attention, and he saw what had happened when the door opened again. Without quite knowing why he did so, he swept the pieces out of the way with his uninjured hand, and a moment later he was left in darkness as the door closed completely. He had an uneasy idea that he was being watched.

Again the voice boomed out. He recognized the word "gold" again, but the syllables which alternated with it were too much distorted for him to understand. He had, after all, no tobacco on his person, and there certainly was none in the torpedo, so that there was nothing to bring the substance to mind. He made no attempt to imitate the alien-sounding word, and after a moment the utterance ceased.

It was replaced by fainter sounds, which somehow did not seem to be directed at him, although they had the complexity of speech. Roger would not, of course, have analyzed them in just that way, but he got the distinct impression that they represented a conversation he could not understand.

This lasted for what seemed to the boy a long time; then the earlier refrain broke out again. "Gold—tofacco—gold—tofacco!" Eventually it got on even Roger's nerves, and he yelled at the dark hulk.

"I don't know what you're saying, darn you! I'm darned if I'll touch your gold again, and I don't know what the other words are. Shut up!" He kicked the hull again, to emphasize his feelings, and was rather startled when the voice fell silent. He backed away a little farther, wondering what this presaged. It was well he did.

An instant later, without preliminary sound, the dark shape of the torpedo lunged upward, crashed through the overhanging branches, and vanished into the black sky with a whistle of protesting air. For minutes the boy stood where he was, gazing up through the gap smashed in the limbs; but nothing rewarded his efforts except the stars.

Roger Wing got very little sleep that night, and the fact that he got his feet wet finding his shelter was only partly responsible.

8

"No, that's not the principal question." Laj Drai repeated the statement rather thoughtfully, as he glided into the shop and absently closed the door behind him.

"Sir, I——" Feth got no farther with his expostulation.

"Oh, don't let me interrupt. Go right ahead, Ken—you have a problem on your hands, I see. Get it out of the way, and we'll tackle the other afterwards. There'll be no interruptions then."

Rather puzzled, for he had completely forgotten Drai's threat, Ken turned back to his microphone and resumed the apparently endless chant. While he did not understand the words with which Roger finally interrupted, the thing had gone on long enough so that he shared the boy's impatience to some extent. Also, the clank as Roger kicked the torpedo was at least suggestive.

It was Drai who drove the projectile into the air, an instant later. He had never heard those words, either; but they were different enough from the usual human conversation to start him shivering. The thought of strained or severed relations with Planet Three was one he could not face—and this being was definitely excited and more than probably angry. That blow on the hull of the torpedo—

Drai's tentacle whipped past Sallman Ken at the thought, and the main power and drive director switches closed as one. The investigator swivelled around on the control rack, and eyed his employer curiously.

"You seem almost as excited as the native. What's the matter?" Laj drew a deep breath, and finally got his voice under control. He was just beginning to realize that his dramatic entry had not been the wisest of moves. It was perfectly possible that his hired expert had learned the name of Earth's product quite innocently; and if that were the case he would be ill-advised to attach too much weight to the incident—publicly, at least. He shifted ground, therefore, as smoothly as he could.

"Your chemical analysis seems to have encountered complications."

"It would seem so. Apparently your natives are not quite so completely diurnal as you gave me to understand." Ken was not intentionally defending his actions, but he could have found no better answer. Laj Drai paused momentarily.

"Yes, that is a point that surprises me a little. For twenty years they have never signalled except during their daytime. I wonder if the flatlanders had anything to do with it? I can't imagine what or how, though. Did you finish your tests?"

"Enough, I guess. We'll have to bring the torpedo back here, so I can find out just what that atmosphere did to my samples. Some of them burned, we already know, but I'd like to know what was produced."

"Of course it couldn't be sulfides. That's what one thinks of as the natural product of combustion."

"Not unless frozen sulfur dust is suspended in the atmosphere in tremendous quantities. I hadn't thought of that, though—I'll check for it when the samples come back. Actually, I'm a little bothered by the results so far. I couldn't think of anything gaseous at that temperature which would support combustion, and something definitely does."

"How about fluorine?" Laj was digging in the dim memories of an elementary science course.

"Maybe—but how come it exists free in the atmosphere? I should think it would be *too* active, even at that temperature. Of course, I suppose the same would be true of anything which would support combustion, so we'll simply have to wait until the samples are back. You know, I'm almost at the point where I'd be willing to risk a landing there, to *see* what the place is like." Drai shrugged expressively.

"If you and Feth can figure out a way of doing it, I won't stop you. We might even see our way to offering a bonus. Well, it'll be nearly three days before your stuff is back here, and there won't be much to do in the meantime. Feth will cut it in on the beam when it's far enough from Three."

Ken took this as a hint to leave, and drifted aimlessly out into the corridors. He had some thinking of his own to do. As Drai had said, nothing could be done about Planet Three until the return of the torpedo, and he had no excuse for not considering Rade's problem for a while.

The product was called "tofacco." That, at least, was information. Rade had had no name for the narcotic he sought, so the information was of questionable value so far.

This planetary system was relatively close to Sarr. Another fact. The precautions taken by Drai and his people to conceal that fact might or might not be considered reasonable for a near-legal commercial enterprise, but were certainly natural for anything as blatantly criminal as drug-running.

Planet Three was cold—to put it feebly—and the drug in question could not stand normal temperatures. That was a link of rather uncertain strength, reinforced slightly by Drai's tacit admission that "tofacco" was a vegetable product.

Think as he would, he could recall no other information which could be of the slightest use to Rade. Ken was mildly annoyed at the narcotics chief anyway for involving him in such a matter, and was certainly more willing than a professional policeman would have been to go back to the purely astronomical and ecological problem that was facing him.

How about his pesky Planet Three? Certainly it was inhabited—a fantastic enough fact in itself. Certainly it was not well known; no vision transmitter and no manned ship had ever gotten through its atmosphere. That seemed a little queer, now that Ken considered the matter again. Granted the fearful cold, and the fact that an atmosphere would conduct heat away as space could not, he still found it hard to believe that a competent engineer could not design apparatus capable of the descent. Feth was supposed to be a mechanic rather than an engineer, of course; but still it seemed very much as though the organization were singularly lacking in scientific resource. The very fact that Ken himself had been hired made that fact even more evident.

Perhaps he was not so far from Rade's problem after all. Certainly any regular interstellar trading organization could and always did have its own ecological staff—no such concern could last without one, considering the rather weird situations apt to arise when, for example, metal-rich Sarr traded with the amphibious chemistry wizards of Rehagh. Yet he, Sallman Ken, a general science dabbler, was all that Laj Drai could get! It was not strange; it was unbelievable. He wondered how Drai had made the fact seem reasonable even for a moment.

Well, if he found out nothing they would probably not bother him. He could and would investigate Planet Three as completely as he could, go home, and turn his information over to Rade—let the narcotics man do what he wanted with it. Planet Three was more interesting.

How to land on the blasted planet? He could see keeping large ships out of its atmosphere, after the trouble with the natives of the flat, bluish areas. Still, torpedoes had been running the gauntlet without loss for twenty years, and the only detectable flatlander activity had been radar beams in the last two or three. Those were easily fooled by quarter wave coatings, as Drai had said. No, the only real objections were the frightful natural conditions of the world.

Well, a standard suit of engineer's armor would let a Sarrian work in a lake of molten aluminum for quite a while. There, of course, the temperature difference was less than it would be on the Planet of Ice; but the conductivity of the metal must be greater than that of the planet's atmosphere, and might make up the difference. Even if it did not, the armor could be given extra heating coils or insulation or both. Why had this never been tried? He would have to ask Feth or Laj Drai.

Then, granting for the moment that a landing could not be made even this way, why was television impossible? Ken refused to believe that the thin glass of a television tube could not be cooled down sufficiently to match the world's conditions without shattering, even if the electrical parts had to be kept hot. Surely the difference could be no greater than in the ancient incandescent bulbs!

He would have to put both these points up to Feth. He was heading purposefully back toward the shop with this plan in mind, when he encountered Drai, who greeted him as though there had been no suspicious thoughts in his own brain that day.

"Feth has cut you in to the main beam, and no piloting will be needed for nearly three days," he said. "You looked as though you were going back to your controls."

"I wanted to talk to Feth again. I've been thinking over the matter of armor and apparatus withstanding Planet Three's conditions, and it seems to me something could be done." He went on to give a censored version of his recent thoughts to his employer.

"I don't know," the latter said when he had finished. "You'll have to talk to Feth, as you planned. We've tried it, since he joined us, and the failures occurred just as he said in the matter of television. He was not with us on the original expedition, which did no investigating except as I originally told you—it was strictly a pleasure cruise, and the only reason there were so many torpedoes available was that the owner of the ship preferred to do his sightseeing in comfort—he'd send out a dozen at once, when we entered a planetary system, and keep the *Karella* in space until he found something he wanted to see or do personally."

"I've never met him, have I?"

"No—he died long ago. He was pretty old when we hit this place. I inherited the ship and got into this trading business."

"When did Feth join you?"

"A year or two after I got started—he's the oldest in the crew in point of service. He can tell you all about the engineering troubles, you see, and I certainly can't. You'd better see him, if he feels like talking." Without explaining this last remark, Drai disappeared down the corridor. Ken did not wonder at the words—he had already come to regard Feth as a taciturn personality.

The mechanic did not appear to be busy. He was still draped in the rack in front of the torpedo controls, and seemed to be thinking. He rose as Ken entered the room, but said nothing, merely giving the equivalent of a nod of greeting. Not noticing anything unusual in his manner, Ken began immediately to spill forth his ideas. He was allowed to finish without interruption.

"Your points all sound good," the mechanic admitted when he had heard them, "and I certainly can't bring any theory against them. I can merely point out that the tubes do break. If you want to send down a suit of armor full of thermometers and pressure gauges, that's all right with me, but I trust you'll pardon a pessimistic attitude. I used up a lot of good TV equipment in that atmosphere."

"Well, I admit your superior practical knowledge," replied Ken, "but I do think it's worth trying."

"If the instruments read all right, who goes down in the armor the next time? The thought makes my knee-joints stiff. I'm scared of the idea, and don't mind admitting it."

"So am I." Ken remembered the uncontrollable emotion that had swept his being the first time he had seen Planet Three. "It's a ghastly place, beyond doubt; but I still like to find things out, and I'm willing to take a chance on my health to do it."

"Health—huh! You'd be a ready-made memorial statue five seconds after the first pinhole appeared in your suit," retorted the mechanic. "I almost feel it's a dirty trick to send good instruments down into that, even when I know they can take it. Well, I'll break out a suit of armor, if you really want to try it. There are plenty of torpedoes."

"How can you carry it by torpedo? You can't possibly get it inside, surely."

"No; there are rings on the outer hull, and we can clamp the suit to those. We'll just have to be careful and go through the atmosphere more slowly, this time." He glided down the length of the shop to a set of lockers at the far end, and from one of these wrestled a suit of the much-discussed armor into view.

Even under Mercurian gravity it was difficult to handle. Owing to the peculiarities of the Sarrian physique, a greatly superior leverage could be obtained from inside the garment; but even knowing this, Ken began to wonder just what he was going to do if he succeeded in reaching the surface of the massive Planet Three in that metal monstrosity, under nearly four times his present gravity. That thought led to a question.

"Feth, what sort of body chemistry do you suppose these natives have? They move around—presumably—under a whopping gravity in a temperature that should freeze any organic material. Ever thought about it?" The mechanic was silent for some time, as though considering his reply.

"Yes," he said at last, "I'll admit I've thought about it. I'm not sure I want to talk about it, though."

"Why not? The place can't be that repulsive."

"It's not that. You remember what Drai said he'd do if anyone gave you information about the stuff we got from the planet?"

"Yes, vaguely; but what does that have to do with it?"

"Maybe nothing, maybe not. He was pretty sore

about my telling you the name of the stuff. I wouldn't have done it if I'd stopped to think. The situation just seemed to call for a quick answer, so I gave it."

"But your ideas on the native chemistry could hardly tell—or I suppose perhaps they could. Still, Drai knows perfectly well I've never worked for another trading company and I'm not a trader myself—why should I be treated like a commercial spy? I don't care particularly what your stuff is—I'm interested in the planet."

"I don't doubt it. Just the same, if I ever make any more slips like that, please keep whatever you learn to yourself. I thought there'd be a nuclear explosion when Drai walked in with you yelling 'Tofacco!' into the mike."

"He couldn't really do much, though." This was a ranging question; Ken had started to think again.

"Well—" Feth was cautious about his answer—"he's the boss, and this isn't such a bad job. Just do the favor, if you don't mind." He turned back to the armor, with an expression on his face which indicated he was through talking for the time being. Ken found himself unable to get anything definite from the mechanic's answer.

He didn't think about it very hard anyway, for the other problem proved too interesting. Feth was certainly a good mechanic; as good as some rated engineers Ken had known. He had opened the armor completely and removed all the service plates, and started the job by giving it a full overhaul inspection. That completed, he refilled the zinc circulating system and replaced and safetied the plates he had removed, but left the armor itself open. One eye rolled questioningly at the watcher, and he spoke for the first time in two hours.

"Have you any ideas about instrument arrangement? You know best what you want to find out."

"Well, all we really need to know is whether the suit can maintain temperature and pressure. I suppose a single pressure gauge anywhere inside, and thermometers at the extremities, would tell enough. Can you use telemetering instruments, or will we have to wait until this torpedo gets back, too?"

"I'm afraid we'll have to wait. The instruments themselves would be easy enough to install, but the voice transmitter in the armor couldn't handle their messages. I can put a multiple recorder in the body, connect the instruments to that, and arrange so you can turn it on and off by remote control—I'll simply tie it in to one of the suit controls. I suppose you'll want to be able to manipulate the suit heaters, as well?"

"Yes. If it takes anywhere near full power to maintain livable temperature, we ought to know it. I suppose extra heaters could be installed, if necessary?"

"I expect so." For the first time, Feth wore an expression approximating a grin. "I could probably mount blast furnaces on the feet. I'm not so sure you could walk around with them."

"Even if I can't I can at least see."

"If you don't have the same trouble with your visor that I did with TV tubes. Even quartz has its limitations."

"I still think it can take it. Anyway, it won't cost *us* anything to find out. Let's go ahead and mount those instruments—I'm rather curious to see which of us is right. Is this recorder all right?" He took from a cabinet a minute machine whose most prominent feature was the double reel of sensitized tape, and held it up as he spoke. Feth glanced at it.

"Only one record. Get an L-7. You can recognize it by the reel—its tape is about five times as wide. I'm using the single barometer you suggested, and thermometers in head, trunk, one foot, and one sleeve as far out as I can mount it. That leaves a free band on the tape that you can use for anything you want." The mechanic was working as he spoke, clamping tiny instruments from a well-stocked supply cabinet into the places he had mentioned. For a moment Ken wondered whether the existence of this more than adequate instrument stock did not invalidate his argument about the lack of scientific facilities; then he recognized that all the devices were perfectly standard engineering instruments, and represented nothing but a respectable financial outlay. Anyone could buy and almost anyone could use them.

In spite of Feth's evident skill, the job was a long one. They did not sleep, being Sarrians, but even they had to rest occasionally. It was during one of these rests that Ken happened to notice the time.

"Say," he remarked to his companion, "it must be daylight on that part of the planet by now. I wonder if Drai has made his landing yet?"

"Very probably," Feth replied, one eye following Ken's gaze toward the clock. "He is more than likely to be back in space again—he doesn't waste much time as a rule."

"In that case, would I be likely to be skinned for dropping in to the observatory?" Feth gazed at him narrowly for long enough to let Ken regret the question.

"I probably would be if Drai found out I'd encouraged you," was the answer. "I think it would be better if you stayed here. There's plenty for us to do." He rose and returned to his labors, although the rest period had scarcely started. Ken, realizing he did not intend to say any more, joined him.

The work turned out to be timed rather nicely. By the time the armor had survived a one-hour leakage and radiation-loss test in the vacuum of the shadowed airlock, had been clamped to the load rings of another torpedo, and launched into the void on automatic control, the other projectile was on the point of landing. The automatic control, in fact, was necessary—the second missile could not be handled by radio until the first had been docked, since the other controlling station was still being used by Drai to bring his own load back to Mercury.

A single rest period fitted nicely between the launching of the suit and the landing of the mobile laboratory; and Ken was awaiting the latter with eagerness when it finally drifted through the air lock under Feth's expert control. He would have pounced on it at once, but was restrained by a warning cry from the mechanic.

"Hold on! It's not as cold as it was out on Planet Three, but you'll still freeze to it. Look!" A tentacle waved toward the gleaming hull, on which drops of liquid sulfur were condensing, running together and trickling to the floor, where they promptly boiled away again. "Let that stop, first."

Ken stopped obediently, feeling the icy draft pour about his feet, and backed slowly away. The air that reached him was bearable, but the hull of the torpedo must be cold enough to freeze zinc, if it had reached radiative equilibrium for this distance from the sun.

Long minutes passed before the metal was warmed through and the drip of liquid sulfur ceased. Only then did Feth open the cargo door, whereupon the process was repeated. This time the straw-colored liquid made a pool on the floor of the cargo compartment, flooding around the crucibles and making Ken wonder seriously about the purity of his samples. He turned on all the heaters at low strength to get rid of the stuff as fast as possible. Since there was a serious chance of further reaction with the air if a high temperature were attained, he opened the switches again the moment the hissing and bubbling of boiling air ceased; and at last he was free to examine his results. As Roger Wing could have told him, they were quite a sight!

9

Some of the little pots were full; most of these appeared to be unchanged. Others, however, were not. The contents of most of these were easy to find, but Ken could see that they were going to be hard to identify.

A white powder was literally over everything, as Roger had already seen. The yellow flecks of sodium peroxide were turning grayish as they decomposed in the heat. The gold crucible had been pulled from its base, but was otherwise unchanged; the iron had turned black; sodium, magnesium and titanium had disappeared, though the residue in each crucible gave promise that some of the scattered dust could be identified. There was still carbon in the container devoted to that substance, but much less of it than there had been.

All these things, however, interesting and important as they might be, only held the attention of Feth and Ken for a moment; for just inside the cargo door, imprinted clearly in the layer of dust, was a mark utterly unlike anything either had ever seen.

"Feth, dig up a camera somewhere. I'm going to get Drai." Ken was gone almost before the words had left his diaphragm, and for once Feth had nothing to say. His eyes were still fixed on the mark.

There was nothing exactly weird or terrifying about it; but he was utterly unable to keep his mind from the fascinating problem of what had made it. To a creature which had never seen anything even remotely like a human being, a hand print is apt to present difficulties in

interpretation. For all he could tell, the creature might
have been standing, sitting, or leaning on the spot, or
sprawled out in the manner the Sarrians substituted for
the second of those choices. There was simply no telling; the native might be the size of a Sarrian foot, making the mark with his body—or he might have been too
big to get more than a single appendage into the compartment. Feth shook his head to clear it—even he began to realize that his thoughts were beginning to go in
circles. He went to look for a camera.

Sallman Ken burst into the observatory without
warning, but gave Drai no chance to explode. He was
bursting himself with the news of the discovery—a little
too much, in fact, since he kept up the talk all the way
back to the shop. By the time they got there, the actual
sight of the print was something of an anticlimax to
Drai. He expressed polite interest, but little more. To
him, of course, the physical appearance of Earth's natives meant nothing whatever. His attention went to another aspect of the compartment.

"What's all that white stuff?"

"I don't know yet," Ken admitted. "The torpedo just
got back. It's whatever Planet Three's atmosphere does
to the samples I sent down."

"Then you'll know what the atmosphere is before
long? That will be a help. There are some caverns near
the dark hemisphere that we've known about for years,
which we could easily seal off and fill with whatever
you say. Let us know when you find out anything." He
drifted casually out of the shop, leaving Ken rather disappointed. It had been such a fascinating discovery.

He shrugged the feeling off, collected what he could
of his samples without disturbing the print, and bore
them across the room to the bench on which a makeshift chemical laboratory had been set up. As he himself
had admitted, he was not an expert analyst; but compounds formed by combustion were seldom extremely
complex, and he felt that he could get a pretty good
idea of the nature of these. After all, he knew the metals involved—there could be no metallic gases except

hydrogen in Planet Three's atmosphere. Even mercury would be a liquid, and no other metal had a really high vapor pressure even at Sarrian temperature. With this idea firmly in mind like a guiding star, Ken set blithely to work.

To a chemist, the work or a description of it would be interesting. To anyone else, it would be a boringly repetitious routine of heating and cooling, checking for boiling points and melting points, fractionating and filtering. Ken would have been quicker had he started with no preconceived notions; but finally even he was convinced. Once convinced, he wondered why he had not seen it before.

Feth Allmer had returned long since, and photographed the hand print from half a dozen angles. Now, seeing that Ken had stopped working, he roused himself from the rack on which he had found repose and approached the work bench.

"Have you got it, or are you stumped?" he queried.

"I have it, I guess. I should have guessed long ago. It's oxygen."

"What's so obvious about that? Or, for that matter, why shouldn't it be?"

"To the latter question, no reason. I simply rejected it as a possibility at first because it's so active. I never stopped to think that it's little if any more active at that temperature than sulfur is at ours. It's perfectly possible to have it free in an atmosphere—provided there's a process constantly replacing what goes into combination. You need the same for sulfur. Blast it, the two elements are so much alike! I should have thought of that right away!"

"What do you mean—a replacement process?"

"You know we breathe sulfur and form sulfides with our metabolic processes. Mineral-eating life such as most plants, on the other hand, breaks down the sulfides and releases free sulfur, using solar energy for the purpose. Probably there is a similar division of life forms on this planet—one forming oxides and the other breaking them down. Now that I think of it, I believe there are some microorganisms on Sarr that use oxygen instead of sulfur."

"Is it pure oxygen?"

"No—only about a fifth or less. You remember how quickly the sodium and magnesium went out, and what the pressure drop was with them."

"No, I don't, and I can't say that it means much to me anyway, but I'll take your word for it. What else is there in the atmosphere? The titanium took about all of it, I do remember."

"Right. It's either nitrogen or some of its oxides—I can't tell which without better controlled samples for quantity measurement. The only titanium compounds I could find in that mess were oxides and nitrides, though. The carbon oxidized, I guess—the reason there was no pressure change except that due to heat was that the principal oxide of carbon has two atoms of oxygen, and there is therefore no volume change. I should have thought of that, too."

"I'll have to take your word for that, too, I guess. All we have to do, then, is cook up a four-to-one mixture of nitrogen and oxygen and fill the caves the boss mentioned to about two-thirds normal pressure with it?"

"That may be a little oversimplified, but it should be close enough to the real thing to let this tofacco stuff grow—if you can get specimens here alive, to start things off. It would be a good idea to get some soil, too—I don't suppose that powdering the local rock would help much. I may add in passing that I refuse even to attempt analyzing that soil. You'll have to get enough to use." Feth stared.

"But that's ridiculous! We need tons, for a decent-sized plantation!" Sallman Ken shrugged.

"I know it. I tell you clearly that it will be easier to get those tons than to get an accurate soil analysis out of me. I simply don't know enough about it, and I doubt if Sarr's best chemist could hazard a prediction about the chemicals likely to be present in the solid state on that planet. At that temperature, I'll bet organic

compounds could exist without either fluorine or sili-
con."

"I think we'd better get Drai back here to listen to
that. I'm sure he was planning to have you synthesize
both atmosphere and soil, so that we could set up the
plantation entirely on our own."

"Perhaps you'd better. I told him my limitations at
the beginning; if he still expects that, he had no idea
whatever of the nature of the problem." Feth left, looking worried, though Ken was unable to understand what
particular difference it made to the mechanic. Later he
was to find out.

The worried expression was still more evident when
Feth returned.

"He's busy now. He says he'll talk it over with you
after that suit comes back, so that any alternatives can
be considered, too. He wants me to take you out to the
caves so you can see for yourself what he has in mind
for making them usable."

"How do we get there? They must be some distance
from here."

"Ordon Lee will take us around in the ship. It's
about two thousand miles. Let's get into our suits."

Ken heroically swallowed the impulse to ask why the
whole subject should have come up so suddenly in the
midst of what seemed a totally different matter, and
went to the locker where the space suits were stowed.
He more than suspected the reason, anyway, and
looked confidently forward to having the trip prolonged
until after the return of the trading torpedo.

His attention was shifted from these matters as he
stepped onto the surface of Mercury, for the first time
since his arrival at the station. The blistered, baked, utterly dry expanse of the valley was not particularly
strange to him, since Sarr was almost equally dry and
even hotter; but the blackness of the sky about the sun
and the bareness of the ground contributed to a *dead*
effect that he found unpleasant. On Sarr, plant life is
everywhere in spite of the dryness; the plants with
which Ken was familiar were more crystalline than or-

ganic and needed only the most minute amounts of liquid for their existence.

Also, Sarr has weather, and Mercury does not. As
the ship lifted from the valley, Ken was able to appreciate the difference. Mercury's terrain is rugged, tower-
ing and harsh. The peaks, faults and meteor scars are
unsoftened by the blurring hand of erosion. Shadows
are dark where they exist at all, relieved only by light
reflected from nearby solid objects. Lakes and streams
would have to be of metals like lead and tin, or simple
compounds like the "water" of Sarr—copper chloride,
lead bromide, and sulfides of phosphorus and potassium. The first sort are too heavy, and have filtered
down through the rocks of Mercury, if they ever existed
at all; the second are absent for lack of the living organ-
isms that might have produced them. Sallman Ken,
watching the surface over which they sped, began to
think a little more highly even of Earth.

A vessel capable of exceeding the speed of light by a
factor of several thousand makes short work of a trip of
two thousand miles, even when the speed is kept down
to a value that will permit manual control. The surface
was a little darker where they landed, with the sun near
the horizon instead of directly overhead and the shadows correspondingly longer. It looked and was colder.
However, the vacuum and the poor conducting qualities
of the rock made it possible even here to venture out in
ordinary space suits, and within a few moments Ken,
Feth and the pilot were afoot gliding swiftly toward a
cliff some forty feet in height.

The rock surface was seamed and cracked, like
nearly all Mercurian topography. Into one of the wider
cracks Lee unhesitatingly led the way. It did not lead
directly away from the sun, and the party found itself
almost at once in utter darkness. With one accord they
switched on their portable lamps and proceeded. The
passage was rather narrow at first, and rough enough
on both floor and walls to be dangerous to space suits.
This continued for perhaps a quarter of a mile, and
quite suddenly opened into a vast, nearly spherical

chamber. Apparently Mercury had not always been without gases—the cave had every appearance of a bubble blown in the igneous rock. The crack through which the explorers had entered extended upward nearly to its top, and downward nearly as far. It had been partly filled with rubble from above, which was the principal reason the going had been so difficult. The lower part of the bubble also contained a certain amount of loose rock. This looked as though it might make a climb down to the center possible, but Ken did not find himself particularly entranced by the idea.

"Is there just this one big bubble?" he asked. Ordon Lee answered.

"No; we have found several, very similar in structure, along this cliff, and there are probably others with no openings into them. I suppose they could be located by echo-sounders if we really wanted to find them."

"It might be a good idea to try that," Ken pointed out. "A cave whose only entrance was one we had drilled would be a lot easier to keep airtight than this thing." Feth and Lee grunted assent to that. The latter added a thought of his own. "It might be good if we could find one well down; we could be a lot freer in drilling—there'd be no risk of a crack running to the surface."

"Just one trouble," put in Feth. "Do we have an echo-sounder? Like Ken on his soil analysis, I have my doubts about being able to make one." Nobody answered that for some moments.

"I guess I'd better show you some of the other caves we've found already," Lee said at last. No one objected to this, and they retraced their steps to daylight. In the next four hours they looked at seven more caves, ranging from a mere hemispherical hollow in the very face of the cliff to a gloomy, frighteningly deep bubble reached by a passageway just barely negotiable for a space-suited Sarrian. This last, in spite of the terrors of its approach and relative smallness, was evidently the best for their purpose out of those examined; and Lee made a remark to that effect as they doffed space suits back in the *Karella*.

"I suppose you're right," Ken admitted, "but I'd still like to poke deeper. Blast it, Feth, are you sure you couldn't put a sounder together? You never had any trouble with the gadgets we used in the torpedoes."

"Now you're the one who doesn't realize the problem," the mechanic replied. "We were using heating coils, thermometers, pressure gauges, and photocells for the other stuff. Those come ready made. All I did was hook them up to a regular achronic transmitter—we couldn't use ordinary radio because the waves would have taken ten or twelve minutes for the round trip. I didn't make anything—just strung wires."

"I suppose you're right," Ken admitted. "In that case, we may as well go back to the station and lay plans for sealing off that last cavern." He kept a sharp look on his two companions as he said this, and succeeded in catching the glance Feth sent at the clock before his reply. It almost pleased him.

"Hadn't we better get some photographs and measurements of the cave first?" Ordon Lee cut in. "We'll need them for estimates on how much gas and soil will be needed, regardless of how it's to be obtained." Ken made no objection to this; there was no point in raising active suspicion, and he had substantiated his own idea. He was being kept away from the station intentionally. He helped with the photography, and subsequently with the direct measurement of the cave. He had some trouble refraining from laughter; affairs were so managed that the party had returned to the ship and doffed space suits each time before the next activity was proposed. It was very efficient, from one point of view. Just to keep his end up, he proposed a rest before returning to the base, and was enthusiastically seconded by the others. Then he decided to compute the volume of the cave from their measurements, and contrived to spend a good deal of time at that—legitimately, as the cave was far from being a perfect sphere. Then he suggested getting some samples of local rock to permit an estimate of digging difficulties, and bit back a grin when Feth suggested rather impatiently that that could wait. Apparently he had outdone the precious pair at their own game—though why Feth should care whether or not they stayed longer than necessary was hard to see.

"It's going to take quite a lot of gas," he said as the *Karella* lunged into the black sky. "There's about two million cubic feet of volume there, and even the lower pressure we need won't help much. I'd like to find out if we can get oxygen from those rocks; we should have picked up a few samples, as I suggested. We're going to have to look over the upper area for small cracks, too— we have no idea how airtight the darn thing is. I wish we could—say, Feth, aren't there a lot of radar units of one sort or another around here?"

"Yes, of course. What do you want them for? Their beams won't penetrate rock."

"I know. But can't the pulse-interval on at least some of them be altered?"

"Of course. You'd have to use a different set every time your range scale changed, otherwise. So what?"

"Why couldn't we—or you, anyway—set one up with the impulse actuating a sounder of some sort which could be put in contact with the rock, and time *that* return-echo picked up by a contact-mike? I know the impulse rate would be slower, but we could calibrate it easily enough."

"One trouble might be that radar units are usually not very portable. Certainly none of the warning devices in this ship are."

"Well, dismantle a torpedo, then. They have radar altimeters, and there are certainly enough of them so one can be spared. We could have called base and had them send one out to us—I bet it would have taken you only a few hours. Let's do that anyway—we're still a lot closer to the caves than to the base."

"It's easier to work in the shop; and anyway, if we go as far underground as this idea should let us— supposing it works—we might as well scout areas closer to the base, for everyone's convenience." Ordon Lee contributed the thought without looking from his controls.

"Do you think you can do it?" Ken asked the mechanic.

"It doesn't seem too hard," the latter answered. "Still, I don't want to make any promises just yet."

"There's a while yet before that suit comes back. We can probably find out before then, and really have some material for Drai to digest. Let's call him now—maybe he'll have some ideas about soil."

The eyes of the other two met for a brief moment; then Lee gestured to the radio controls.

"Go ahead; only we'll be there before you can say much."

"He told me you were going to manufacture soil," reminded Feth.

"I know. That's why I want to talk to him— we left in too much of a hurry before." Ken switched on the radio while the others tried to decide whether or not he was suspicious about that hasty departure. Neither dared speak, with Ken in the same room, but once again their eyes met, and the glances were heavy with meaning.

Drai eventually came to the microphone at the other end and Ken began talking with little preliminary.

"We've made measurements of the smallest cave we can find, so far at least, and figured out roughly how much air you're going to need to fill it. I can tell you how much soil you'll need to cover the bottom, too, if you plan to use all of it. The trouble is, even if I can analyze the soil—even as roughly as I did the air— you're facing a supply problem that runs into tons. I can't make that much in the laboratory in any reasonable time. You're going to have to get it ready-made."

"How? We can't land a person on Planet Three, let alone a freighter."

"That we'll see presently. But that's not the suggestion I wanted to make—I see we're nearly there, so we can finish this chat in person. Think this over while we're going in: whatever sort of atmosphere a planet may have, I don't see how the soils can be *too* different—at least in their principal constituents. Why don't you get a shipload of Sarrian soil?" Drai gaped for a moment.

"But—bacteria—"

"Don't be silly; nothing Sarrian could live at that temperature. I admit it would be safer to use soil from Planet Three, and we may be able to. But if we can't, then you have my advice, if you're interested in speed—even if I knew the composition, it would take me a lot longer than a week to make a hundred tons of dirt!" He broke the connection as the *Karella* settled to the ground.

10

Ken wasted no time donning his space suit and leaving the ship with the others. Once inside the station and out of the heavy garment, he hastened to the shop to see how far out the returning test suit was; then, satisfied with its progress as recorded there, he headed for the observatory to continue his conversation with Laj Drai. He met no one on the way. Lee had stayed on the ship, Feth had disappeared on some errand of his own the moment the lock had closed behind them, and the rest of the personnel kept pretty much to themselves anyway. Ken did not care this time whether or not he were seen, since he planned a perfectly above-board conversation.

He was interrupted, however, in planning just how to

present his arguments, by the fact that the observatory door was locked.

It was the first time he had encountered a locked door in the station since his arrival, and it gave him to think furiously. He was morally certain that the trading torpedo had returned during the absence of the *Karella,* and that there was a load of tofacco somewhere around the building. If this were the only locked door—and it was, after all, the room Drai used as an office—

Ken pressed his body close to the door, trying to tell by sound whether anyone were in the room. He was not sure; and even if there were not, what could he do? A professional detective could probably have opened the door in a matter of seconds. Ken, however, was no professional; the door was definitely locked, as far as he was concerned. Apparently the only thing to do was seek Drai elsewhere.

He was ten yards down the ramp, out of sight of the observatory door, when he heard it open. Instantly he whirled on his toes and was walking back up the incline as though just arriving. Just as he reached the bend that hid the door from him he heard it close again; and an instant later he came face to face with Feth. The mechanic, for the first time since Ken had known him, looked restless and uneasy. He avoided Ken's direct gaze, and wound the tip of one tentacle more tightly about a small object he was carrying, concealing it from view. He brushed past with a muttered greeting and vanished with remarkable speed around the turn of the ramp, making no answer to Ken's query as to whether Drai were in the observatory.

Ken stared after him for seconds after he had disappeared. Feth had always been taciturn, but he had seemed friendly enough. Now it almost seemed as though he were angry at Ken's presence.

With a sigh, the pro tem detective turned back up the ramp. It wouldn't hurt to knock at the door, anyway. The only reason he hadn't the first time was probably a subconscious hope that he would find Drai somewhere else, and feel free to investigate. Since his common sense told him he couldn't investigate anyway, he knocked.

It was just as well he hadn't made any amateur efforts at lock-picking, he decided as the door opened. Drai was there, apparently waiting for him. His face bore no recognizable expression; either whatever bothered Feth had not affected him, or he was a much better actor than the mechanic. Ken, feeling he knew Feth, inclined to the former view.

"I'm afraid I'm not convinced of the usability of any Sarrian soil," Drai opened the conversation. "I agree that most of the substances present in it, as far as I know, could also be present at Planet Three's temperature; but I'm not so sure the reverse is true. Mightn't there be substances that would be solid or liquid at that temperature and gaseous at ours, so that they would be missing from any we brought from home?"

"I hadn't thought of that," Ken admitted. "The fact that I can't think of any such substances doesn't mean they don't exist, either. I can skim through the handbook and see if there are any inorganic compounds that would behave that way, but even that might miss some—and if their life is at all analogous to ours, there are probably a couple of million organic compounds— for which we *don't* have any catalogue. No, blast it, I guess you're right; we'll have to take the stuff from the planet itself." He lapsed into silent thought, from which Drai finally aroused him.

"Do you really think you're going to be able to get to the surface of that world?"

"I still can't see why we shouldn't," replied Ken. "It seems to me that people have visited worse ones before, bad as that is. Feth is pessimistic about it, though, and I suppose he has more practical knowledge of the problem than I. We can make more definite plans in that direction when the suit comes back, which shouldn't be long now. According to the instruments it started back a couple of hours ago."

"That means nearly three days before you're sure. There must be something else—say! You claim it's the presence of a conducting atmosphere that makes the heat loss on Planet Three so great, don't you?"

"Sure. You know as well as I that you can go out in an ordinary space suit light years from the nearest sun; radiation loss is easy to replace. Why?"

"I just thought—there are other planets in this system. If we could find an airless one roughly the same temperature as Three, we might get soil from that."

"That's an idea." Ken was promptly lost in enthusiasm again. "As long as it's cold enough, which is easy in this system—and Three has a satellite—you showed it to me. We can go there in no time in the *Karella*—and we could pick up that suit in space while we're at it. Collect Feth, and let's go!"

"I fear Feth will not be available for a while," replied Drai. "Also," he grimaced, "I have been on that satellite, and its soil is mostly pumice dust; it might have come straight from the Polar Desert on Sarr. We'd better consider the other possibilities before we take off. The trouble is, all we've ever noted about the other planets of the system is their motions. We wanted to avoid them, not visit them. I do remember, I think, that Five and Six do have atmospheres, which I suppose writes them off the list. You might see where Four is just now, will you? I assume you can interpret an ephemeris."

Ken decided later that courtesy was really a superfluous facet of character. Had it not been for the requirements of courtesy he would not have bothered to make an answer to this suggestion, and had not most of his attention been concentrated on the answer he would never have made the serious error of walking over to the cabinet where the table in question was located, and reaching for it. He realized just as he touched the paper what he was doing, but with a stupendous effort of will he finished his assurance that he could read an ephemeris and completed the motion of obtaining the document. He felt, however, as though a laboratory vacuum pump had gone to work on his stomach as he turned back to his employer.

That individual was standing exactly where he had been, the expression on his face still inscrutable.

"I fear I must have done our friend Feth an injustice," he remarked casually. "I was wondering how you had come to imply that a round trip to Sarr would take only a week. I realize of course that your discoveries were made quite accidentally, and that nothing was farther from your plans than vulgar spying; but the problem of what to do about your unfortunate knowledge remains. That will require a certain amount of thought. In the meantime, let us continue with the matter of Planet Four. Is it in a convenient position to visit, and could we as you suggested pick up the torpedo carrying your suit without going too far from course?"

Ken found himself completely at a loss. Drai's apparently unperturbed blandness was the last attitude he expected under the circumstances. He could not believe that the other was really that indifferent; something unpleasant must be brewing between those steady eyes, but the face gave him no clue. As best he could he tried to match his employer's attitude. With an effort he turned his attention to the ephemeris he was holding, found the proper terms, and indulged in some mental arithmetic.

"The planets are just about at right angles as seen from here," he announced at length. "We're just about between the sun and Three, as you know; Four is in the retrograde direction, roughly twice as far from us. Still, that shouldn't mean anything to the *Karella*."

"True enough. Very well, we will take off in an hour. Get any equipment you think you will need on board before then—better use engineering armor for Planet Four, even if it doesn't have air. You'll have to point out where they are to whomever I get to help you."

"How about Feth?" Ken had gotten the idea that the mechanic was in disgrace for betraying the secret of their location.

"He won't be available for some time—he's occupied. I'll give you a man—you can be picking out what you want in the shop; I'll send him there. One hour." Laj

Drai turned away, intimating that the interview was at an end.

The man he sent proved to be a fellow Ken had seen around, but had never spoken to. The present occasion did little to change that; he was almost as taciturn as Feth, and Ken never did learn his name. He did all he was asked in the way of moving material to the *Karella*, and then disappeared. The takeoff was on schedule.

Ordon Lee, who evidently had his orders, sent the vessel around the planet so rapidly that the acceleration needed to hug the curving surfaces exceeded that produced by the planet's gravity; the world seemed to be above them, to the inhabitants of the ship. With the sun near the horizon behind and the glowing double spark of Earth rising ahead, however, he discontinued the radial acceleration and plunged straight away from the star. Under the terrific urge of the interstellar engines, the Earth-Luna system swelled into a pair of clearly marked discs in minutes. Lee applied his forces skilfully, bringing the vessel to a halt relative to the planet and half a million miles sunward of it. Drai gestured to Ken, indicating a control board similar to that in the shop.

"That's tuned in to your torpedo; the screen at the right is a radar unit you can use to help find it. There's a compass at the top of the panel, and this switch will cause the torpedo to emit a homing signal." Ken silently placed himself at the controls, and got the feel of them in a few minutes. The compass gave rather indefinite readings at first because of the distance involved; but Lee was quickly able to reduce that, and in a quarter of an hour the still invisible projectile was only a dozen miles away. Ken had no difficulty in handling it from that point, and presently he and Drai left the control room and repaired to a cargo chamber in the *Karella*'s belly, where the torpedo was warming up.

This time it was the suit still clamped to the outside that took all their interest. The whole thing had been left at the bottom of the atmosphere for a full hour, and Ken felt that any serious faults should be apparent in that time. It was a little discouraging to note that air was condensing on the suit as well as the hull; if the heaters had been working properly, some sort of equilibrium should have been reached between the inner and outer layers of the armor during the few hours in space. More accurately, since an equilibrium had undoubtedly been reached, it should have been at a much higher temperature.

The trickling of liquid air did cease much sooner on the armor, however, and Ken still had some hope when he was finally able to unclamp the garment and take it in for closer examination.

The outer surface of the metal had changed color. That was the first and most obvious fact. Instead of the silvery sheen of polished steel, there was a definitely bluish tint on certain areas, mostly near the tips of the armlike handling extensions and the inner surfaces of the legs. Ken was willing to write off the color as a corrosion film caused by the oxygen, but could not account for its unequal distribution. With some trepidation he opened the body section of the massive suit, and reached inside.

It was cold. Too cold for comfort. The heating coils might have been able to overcome that, but they were not working. The recorder showed a few inches of tape—it had been started automatically by a circuit which ran from a pressure gauge in the torpedo through one of the suit radio jacks as soon as atmospheric pressure had been detectable—and that tape showed a clear story. Temperature and pressure had held steady for a few minutes; then, somewhere about the time the torpedo must have reached the planet's surface, or shortly thereafter, they had both started erratically downward—very erratically, indeed; there was even a brief rise above normal temperature. The recorder had been stopped when the temperature reached the freezing point of sulfur, probably by air solidifying around its moving parts. It had not resumed operation. The planet was apparently a heat trap, pure and simple.

There was no direct evidence that the suit had leaked

gas either way, but Ken rather suspected it had. The bluish tint on portions of the metal might conceivably be the result of flame—flaming oxygen, ignited by jets of high-pressure sulfur coming from minute leaks in the armor. Both sulfur and oxygen support combustion, as Ken well knew, and they do combine with each other— he made a mental note to look up the heats of formation of any sulfides of oxygen that might exist.

He turned away from the debacle at last.

"We'll let Feth look this over when we get back," he said. "He may have better ideas about just how and why the insulation failed. We may as well go on to Planet Four and see if it has anything that might pass for soil."

"We've been orbiting around it for some time, I imagine," Drai responded. "Lee was supposed to head that way as soon as we got your suit on board, but he was not to land until I returned to the control room." The two promptly glided forward, pulling their weightless bodies along by means of the grips set into the walls, and shot within seconds through the control room door—even Ken was getting used to non-standard gravity and even to none at all.

Drai's assumption proved to be correct; drive power was off, and Mars hung beyond the ports. To Sarrian eyes it was even more dimly lighted than Earth, and like it obviously possessed of an atmosphere. Here, however, the atmospheric envelope was apparently less dense. They were too close to make out the so-called canals, which become river valleys when observation facilities are adequate, but even rivers were something new to the Sarrians. They were also too close to see the polar caps from their current latitude, but as the *Karella* drifted southward a broad expanse of white came into view. The cap was nowhere near the size it had been two months before, but again it was a completely strange phenomenon to the gazing aliens.

Or, more accurately, almost completely strange. Ken tightened a tentacle about one of Drai's.

"There was a white patch like that on Planet Three!

I remember it distinctly! There's *some* resemblance between them, anyway."

"There are two, as a matter of fact," replied Drai. "Do you want to get your soil from there? We have no assurance that it is there that the tofacco grows on Planet Three."

"I suppose not; but I'd like to know what the stuff is anyway. We can land at the edge of it, and get samples of everything we find. Lee?"

The pilot looked a little doubtful, but finally agreed to edge down carefully into atmosphere. He refused to commit himself to an actual landing until he had found how rapidly the air could pull heat from his hull. Neither Drai nor Ken objected to this stipulation, and presently the white, brown and greenish expanse below them began to assume the appearance of a landscape instead of a painted disc hanging in darkness.

The atmosphere turned out to be something of a delusion. With the ship hanging a hundred feet above the surface, the outside pressure gauges seemed very reluctant to move far from zero. Pressure was about one fiftieth of Sarr normal. Ken pointed this out to the pilot, but Ordon Lee refused to permit his hull to touch ground until he had watched his outside pyrometers for fully fifteen minutes. Finally satisfied that heat was not being lost any faster than it could be replaced, he settled down on a patch of dark-colored sand, and listened for long seconds to the creak of his hull as it adapted itself to the changed load and localized heat loss. At last, apparently satisfied, he left his controls and turned to Ken.

"If you're going out to look this place over, go ahead. I don't think your armor will suffer any worse than our hull. If you have trouble anywhere, it will be with your feet—loss through the air is nothing to speak of. If your feet get cold, though, don't waste time—get back inside!"

Ken cast a mischievous glance at Drai. "Too bad we didn't bring two suits," he said. "I'm sure you'd have liked to come with me."

"Not in a hundred lifetimes!" Drai said emphatically. Ken laughed outright. Curiously enough, his own original horror of the fearful chill of these Solar planets seemed to have evaporated; he actually felt eager to make the test. With the help of Drai and Lee he climbed into the armor they had brought from Mercury, sealed it, and tested its various working parts. Then he entered the air lock of the *Karella,* and observed his instruments carefully while it was pumped out. Still nothing appeared to be wrong, and he closed the switch actuating the motor of the outer door.

For some reason, as the Martian landscape was unveiled before him, his mind was dwelling on the curious discoloration of the suit that had been exposed to Planet Three's atmosphere, and wondering if anything of the sort was likely to happen here.

Curiously enough, one hundred sixty million miles away, a thirteen year old boy was trying to account for a fire which seemed to have burned over a small patch of brush, isolated by bare rock, on a hillside five miles west of his home.

11

Even to an Earth man, Mars is not a world to promote enthusiasm. It is rather cold at the best of times, much too dry, and woefully lacking in air—breathable or otherwise. The first and last of these points struck Ken most forcibly.

The landscape in front of him was very flat. It was also very patchy. In some spots bare rock showed, but those were few and far between. Much of the area seemed to be dark, naked soil, with bits of green, brown, red and yellow mingling in the general background. Nearly half of the landscape seemed to be composed of the patches of white, which had seemed to be a solid mass from space. Probably, Ken realized, they formed a solid covering closer to the center of the white region; they had landed on its edge, as planned.

He took a careful step away from the ship's side. The gravity was less than that of Sarr, but distinctly greater than on Mercury, and the armor was a severe burden. The two tentacles inside his right "sleeve" forced the clumsy pipe of steel downward almost to the ground, and manipulated the handlers at the end. With some difficulty, he scraped loose a piece of dark brown soil and raised it to eye level. He locked the "knees" of the armor and settled back on the tail-like prop that extended from the rear of the metal trunk, so that he could give all his attention to examining the specimen.

The glass of his face plate showed no signs of differential contraction so far, but he carefully avoided letting the soil touch it during the examination. He almost forgot this precaution, however, when he saw the tiny vari-colored objects on the surface of the sample. Weird as they were in shape, they were unquestionably plants—tiny, oddly soft-looking compared to the crystalline growths of Sarr, but still plants. And they lived in this frightful cold! Already those nearest the metal of his handler were shrivelling and curling, cold as the outside of his armor already must be. Eagerly Ken reported this to the listeners inside.

"This life must have something in common with that of Three," he added. "Both must run on chemical energy of the same general sort, since there's no important difference in their temperatures. This soil must have all the elements necessary, even if the compounds aren't quite right for what we want—who ever heard of a life form that didn't have a good deal of latitude that way?" He looked back at the sample he was holding. "It looks a little different around the edges, as though the heat of my armor were making some change in it. You may be right, Drai—there may be some volatile substance in this soil that's evaporating now. I wonder if I can trap it?" He lapsed into thought, dropping his specimen.

"You can try afterward. Why not investigate the white patches?" called Drai. "And the rocks, too; they might be something familiar—and soils are made from rock, after all." Ken admitted the justice of this, hitched himself off the rear prop, unlocked his leg joints, and resumed his walk away from the ship.

So far, he had felt no sign of cold, even in his feet. Evidently the soil was not a very good conductor of heat. That was not too surprising, but Ken made a mental note to be careful of any patches of solid rock he might encounter.

The nearest of the white areas was perhaps thirty yards from the air lock door. Reaching it quickly enough in spite of the weight of his armor, Ken looked it over carefully. He could not bend over to examine its texture, and was a little uneasy about picking it up; but remembering that the handlers of his armor extended some distance beyond the actual tips of his tentacles, as well as the fact that the first sample had been harmless, he reached down and attempted to scrape up a piece.

This seemed easy enough. The handler grated across the surface, leaving a brown streak behind—evidently the white material formed a very thin layer on the ground. Raising the sample to eye level, however, Ken discovered that he had nothing but dark-colored sand.

Excusably puzzled, he repeated the process, and this time was quick enough to see the last of the white material vanish from the sand grains. "You were right, Laj," he said into his transmitter. "There's something here that's really volatile. I haven't got enough for a good look, yet—I'll try to find a deeper deposit." He started forward again, toward the center of the white patch.

The expanse was perhaps fifty yards across, and Ken judged that the volatile coating might be thicker in the center. This proved to be the case, but it never became heavy enough to impede even his progress. His trail was clearly marked by bare soil, as the stuff faded eerily out of sight around each footprint. Ken, though he could have looked behind in his armor without turning his whole body, did not notice this, but the watchers from the ship did. Drai remarked on it over the radio, and Ken responded:

"Tell me if it stops—maybe that will be a place where it's thick enough to pick some of the stuff up. I'd like to get a close look at it before it evaporates. Right now, I can't imagine what it might be, and I need information badly in order to make even an educated guess."

"The trail is getting narrower now—there are separate spots which outline the shape of the feet of your armor, instead of broad circular areas that blend into each other. A little farther ought to do it."

A little farther did. Ken was not quite to the center of the white patch when Drai reported that he had ceased to leave a trail. He promptly stopped, propped himself as he had before, and scooped up a fresh handful of the evanescent substance. This time there was practically no sand included; the material was fully an inch deep. The mass on his handler began to shrink at once, but not so rapidly as to prevent his getting a fairly long look. It was crystalline, millions of minute facets catching and scattering the feeble sunlight; but the individual crystals were too tiny to permit him to determine their shape. It was gone before he was really satisfied, but there seemed little likelihood of his getting a better look. Somehow a sample would have to be obtained—and analyzed. He thought he saw how that might be done, but some careful preparation would be necessary. Announcing this fact over his suit radio, he prepared to return to the ship.

Perhaps, in the half-seated attitude he had been holding, his feet had been partly out of contact with the armor; perhaps in his single-minded interest in things outside he simply had not noticed what was happening. Whatever the cause, it was not until he stood up that the abrupt, stabbing blade of cold seared straight from his feet to his brain. For an instant he settled back on

his prop, trying to draw his feet from the biting touch of
what was supposed to be insulation; then, realizing that
matters would only grow worse if he delayed, he forced
himself into action. Barely able to bite back a scream of
anguish, he strained every muscle forcing the unwieldy
mass of metal toward the air lock; and even through his
pain, the thought came driving—no wonder the trail
had become narrower; the feet of his armor must be
nearly at the temperature of their surroundings. From
five hundred degrees above zero Centigrade to fifty below is quite a temperature gradient for a scant three
inches of steel, vacuum space, fluid coils, and insulating
fiber to maintain, even with a powerful heating coil
backing up the high-temperature side of the barrier.

The pain grew less as he struggled toward the lock,
but the fact did not make him any happier; it terrified
him. If he should lose control of his feet, he would die
within sight of the *Karella*'s crew, for there was not another suit of special armor aboard that could be worn to
rescue him.

Now his face was cold, too—he must be losing radiation even through the special glass of the face plate. His
tentacle tips were feeling the chill, but not so badly; the
fact that the deadly whiteness had touched only the
handlers, inches beyond the "inhabited" parts of the
sleeve, was helping there. He had reached the edge of
the area of death, and only thirty yards of bare ground
lay between him and the lock. That ground was cold,
too. It must be as cold as the other area; but at least it
did not seem to drink heat. The lock door was open as
he had left it, a metal-lined cavern that seemed to draw
away as he struggled forward. He was numb below the
lower knees, now; for the first time he blessed the
clumsy stiffness of the armor legs, which made them
feel and act like stilts, for that was all that enabled him
to control the feet. Once he stumbled, and had time to
wonder if he would ever be able to get the clumsy bulk
erect again; then he had caught himself in some way—
he never learned how, and no one on the ship could tell
him—and was reeling forward again. Ten yards to go—

five—two—and he brought up against the hull of the
Karella with a clang. One more step and he was inside
the lock. Two, and he was out of the swing of the massive door. With frantic haste he swung the sleeve of his
armor at the closing switch. He hit it—hit it hard
enough to bend the toggle, but the circuit was closed
and the door thudded shut behind him, the sound of its
closing coming through the metal of floor and suit.
Then came the air, automatically, pouring into the lock
chamber, condensing on the body of his armor, freezing
into a yellow crust on the extremities. With the pressure
up, the inner door swung wide, revealing Drai and Ordon Lee in the corridor beyond. The former shrank
from the fierce chill that poured from the chamber; the
pilot, thinking faster, leaped to a locker nearby and
seized a welding torch. Playing the flame of this ahead
of him, he approached Ken carefully.

The crust of sulfur boiled away instantly in the
flame, to be replaced almost as fast when the tongue of
light swung elsewhere. Long seconds passed before the
metal was warm enough to stay clear, and more before
it could be touched, and the almost unconscious Ken
extracted. Minutes more passed before the throbbing
agony receded from his limbs, and he was able to talk
coherently, but at last he was satisfied that no permanent damage had been done. He had not actually been
frost-bitten, though judging by the color of his skin he
had come dangerously near to it.

Drai and Lee, amazed and horrified at the results of
the brief sortie, felt both emotions redoubled as they
heard of his plans for another. Even Drai, interested as
he was in obtaining useful information, made a half-
hearted attempt to dissuade him from the project. Ken
refused to be dissuaded, and his employer did not have
too much difficulty in consoling himself—after all, it
was Ken's health.

The instructions to bring "whatever he thought he
would need" had been obeyed, and Ken spent some
time searching through the pile of apparatus from the
Mercurian laboratory. What he found seemed to satisfy

him, and he made a number of careful preparations which involved some very precise weighing. He then carried several items of equipment to the air lock, and finally donned the armor again, to Ordon Lee's undisguised admiration.

From the control room port, Drai and the pilot watched Ken's hasty trip back to the scene of his earlier trouble. He followed his earlier trail, which was still clearly visible, and carefully avoided touching the whiteness with any part of his armor. Arrived at the point where his cooling boots had been unable to boil their way down to solid ground, he stopped. The watchers were unable to make out his actions in detail, but apparently he set some object on the ground, and began rolling it about as the white substance evaporated from around it. Presently this ceased to happen, as its temperature fell to that of its surroundings; then Ken appeared to pick it up and separate it into two parts. Into one of these he scooped a quantity of the mysterious stuff, using an ordinary spoon. Then the two halves of the thing were fastened together again, and the scientist beat a hasty retreat toward the air lock.

Drai was promptly headed for the inner door of the chamber, expecting to see what was going on; but the portal remained closed. He heard the hissing of air as pressure was brought up, and then nothing. He waited for some minutes, wondering more and more, and finally went slowly back to the control room. He kept looking back as he went, but the valve remained sealed.

As he entered the control room, however, Lee had something to report.

"He's pumping the lock down again," the pilot said, gesturing to a flaring violet light on the board. Both Sarrians turned to the port of the side toward the air lock, Lee keeping one eye on the indicator that would tell them when the outer door opened. It flashed in a matter of seconds, and the watchers crowded eagerly against the transparent panel, expecting Ken's armored figure to appear. Again, however, nothing seemed to happen.

"What in the Galaxy is the fellow up to?" Drai asked the world at large, after a minute or so. Lee treated the question as rhetorical, but did shift part of his attention back to the control board. Even here, however, fully five minutes passed without anything occurring; then the outer door closed again. Calling Drai's attention to this, he looked expectantly at the pressure indicator, which obediently flashed a report of rising pressure. They waited no longer, but headed down the corridor side by side.

This time Ken appeared to have finished his work; the inner door was open when they reached it. He had not permitted his suit to get so cold this time, it seemed; only a light dew dimmed its polish. Within a minute or so Lee was able to help him emerge. He was wearing a satisfied expression, which did not escape the watchers.

"You found out what it was!" Drai stated, rather than asked.

"I found out something which will let me figure out what it is, very shortly," replied Ken.

"But what did you do? Why did you go out twice?"

"You must have seen me putting a sample into the pressure bomb. I sealed it in, and brought it inside so it would all evaporate and so that the pressure gauge on the bomb would be at a temperature where I could trust it. I read the pressure at several temperatures, and weighed the bomb with the sample. I had already weighed it empty—or rather, with the near-vacuum this planet uses for air inside it. The second time I opened the door was to let off the sample, and to make a check at the same temperature with a sample of the planet's air—after all, it must have contributed a little to the pressure the first time."

"But what good would all that do?"

"Without going into a lot of detail, it enabled me to find out the molecular weight of the substance. I did not expect that to be very conclusive, but as it happened I think it will be; it's so small that there aren't many possible elements in it—certainly nothing above fluorine, and I think nothing above oxygen. I'll concede that I may be off a unit or so in my determination, since the apparatus and observing conditions were not exactly ideal, but I don't think it can be much worse than that."

"But what is it?"

"The molecular weight? Between eighteen and nineteen, I got."

"What has that weight, though?"

"Nothing at all common. I'll have to look through the handbook, as I said. Only the very rarest elements are that light."

"If they're so rare, maybe the stuff is not so important for life after all." Ken looked at Drai to see if he were serious.

"In the first place," he pointed out, seeing that the other had not been joking, "mere rarity doesn't prove that life doesn't need it. We use quite respectable quantities of fluorine in our bodies, not to mention zinc, arsenic and copper. This other form of life may well do the same. In the second place, just because an element is rare on Sarr doesn't prove it would be so on Planet Three—it's a much bigger world, and could easily have held considerable quantities of the lighter elements during its original formation, even if they had been there as uncombined gases." The group had been walking toward Ken's room, where he had stored most of his apparatus, as they talked. Reaching it at this point, they entered. Ken draped himself without apology on the only rack, and began to flip through the pages of the chemical handbook, in the section devoted to inorganic compounds. He realized that his mysterious substance could contain carbon, but it certainly could not contain more than one atom per molecule, so there was no danger of its being a really complex organic material.

There were, in fact, just eight elements likely to be present; and the laws of chemistry would put considerable restriction on the possible combinations of those eight. The lightest of these was hydrogen, of course; and to the hydrogen compounds Ken turned, since they came first in that section of the handbook.

Drai had moved to a position from which he could

oversee the pages that Ken was reading; the less interested or less excitable Lee stayed near the door and waited silently. He was more prepared than his employer for a long wait while the scientist made his search; and he was correspondingly more surprised when Ken, almost as soon as he began reading, suddenly stiffened in a fashion which indicated he had found something of interest. Drai saw the action as well.

"What is it?" he asked at once. Both Ken and Lee realized that the "it" referred to the substance, not the cause of Ken's interest; Drai assumed without thought that his scientist had found what he was seeking.

"Just a moment. There's something that doesn't quite agree—but the rest is too perfect—wait a minute—" Ken's voice trailed off for a moment; then, "Of course. This is under normal pressure." He looked up from the book.

"This appears to be the stuff—it's almost completely unknown on Sarr, because of its low molecular weight—most of it must have escaped from the atmosphere eons ago, if it ever was present. According to this handbook, it should be liquid through quite a temperature range, but that's under our atmospheric pressure. It's quite reasonable that it should sublime the way it did in this vacuum."

"But what is it?"

"One of the oxides of hydrogen—H_2O, apparently. If it proves to be essential for the form of growth you're interested in, we're going to have a very interesting time handling it."

"We have cargo shells that can be kept at outside conditions, and towed outside the ship," Drai pointed out.

"I assumed you did," replied Ken. "However, normal 'outside' conditions in the space near Planet One would almost certainly cause this stuff to volatilize just as it did from the comparatively faint heat radiating from my armor. Your shells will have to be sealed airtight, and you will, as I said, have an interesting time transferring their contents to any cave we may pick."

Laj Drai looked startled for several seconds. Then he appeared to remember something, and his expression changed to one of satisfaction.

"Well," he said, "I'm sure you'll be able to figure that one out. That's what scientists are for, aren't they?" It was Ken's turn to look startled, though he had known Drai long enough by this time to have expected something of the sort.

"Don't you ever solve your own problems?" he asked, a trifle sourly. Drai nodded slowly.

"Yes, sometimes. I like to think them over for quite a while, though, and if they're scientific ones I don't have the knowledge to think with. That's why I hire people like you and Feth. Thanks for reminding me—I do have a problem at the moment, on which I have spent a good deal of thought. If you'll excuse me, I'll attend to the finishing touches. You can stay here and work on this one."

"There's nothing more we can do on this planet for the present."

"That I can believe. We'll head back for Planet One and the rest of your laboratory facilities. Come on, Lee—we'll leave the scientist to his science."

Ken, unsuspicious by nature, did not even look up as the two left his room. He had just found ammonia on the list, and was wondering whether his measurement could have been far enough off to permit the true molecular weight to be only seventeen. Melting-point data finally reassured him. For safety's sake, however, he went through all the hydrogen, lithium, beryllium, boron, nitrogen, and oxygen compounds that were listed in the handbook. The faint disturbance incident to the vessel's takeoff did not bother him at all. The silent opening of his door made no impression on him, either.

In fact, the door had closed again with a crisp snap before anything outside the printed pages registered on his consciousness. Then a voice, coincident with the closing door, suddenly shattered the silence.

"Sallman Ken!" The mechanical speaker over the entrance boomed the words; the voice was that of Laj

Drai. "I said when we parted a moment ago that I occasionally solve my own problems. Unfortunately, you have come to represent a problem. There seems to be only one solution which will not destroy your usefulness. In a way I regret to employ it, but you have really only your own unwarranted curiosity to thank. When you wake up, we will talk again—you can tell me what you think of our commercial product!" The voice ceased, with a click which indicated that the microphone had been switched off.

Ken, fully aroused, had dropped the book and risen to his feet—or rather, left his rack and floated away from the floor, since they were in weightless flight. His eyes roved rapidly to all quarters of the room in search of something that might furnish meaning to Drai's rather ominous words. Several seconds passed before he saw it—a rectangular yellow brick, floating in the air near the door. For a moment he did not recognize it, and pushed against a wall to bring himself nearer to it; then, as he felt the chill emanating from the thing, he tried futilely to check his drift.

Already the brick was losing shape, its corners rounding with the heat and puffing off into vapor. It was frozen sulfur—harmless enough in itself if contact were avoided, but terrifying when considered with his background of knowledge and suspicion. With a frantic flailing of his tentacles, he managed to set up enough of an air current to cause the thing to drift out of his path; but an equally anxious look about the room for something which might serve as a gas mask disclosed nothing.

He found himself unable to take his eyes from the dwindling object, now a rather elongated ellipsoid. It continued to shrink remorselessly, and suddenly there was something else visible in the yellow—the end of a small white cylinder. As the last of the protective box vanished, this began to turn brown and then black over its entire surface, and a spherical cloud of smoke enveloped it. For an instant a wild hope flashed in Ken's mind; the thing had to burn, and a fire will not maintain itself in weightless flight. It requires a forced draft. Perhaps this one would smother itself out—but the cloud of smoke continued to swell. Apparently the thing had been impregnated with chips of frozen air in anticipation of this situation.

Now the edges of the smoke cloud were becoming fuzzy and ill-defined as diffusion carried its particles through the room. Ken caught the first traces of a sweetish odor, and tried to hold his breath; but he was too late. The determination to make the effort was his last coherent thought.

12

"So they decided to keep you." There might or might not have been a faint trace of sympathy in Feth Allmer's tone. "I'm not very surprised. When Drai raised a dust storm with me for telling you how far away Sarr was, I knew you must have been doing some probing on your own. What are you, Commerce or Narcotics?" Ken made no answer.

He was not feeling much like talking, as a matter of fact. He could remember just enough of his drug-induced slumber to realize things about himself which no conscientious being should be forced to consider. He had dreamed he was enjoying sights and pleasures whose recollection now gave him only disgust—and yet under the disgust was the hideous feeling that there had been pleasure, and there might be pleasure again. There is no real possibility of describing the sensations of a drug addict, either while he is under the influence of his narcotic or during the deadly craving just before the substance becomes a physical necessity; but at this moment, less than an hour after he had emerged from its influence, there may be some chance of his frame of mind being understandable. Feth certainly understood, but apparently chose not to dwell on that point.

"It doesn't matter now which you were, or whether the whole gang knows it," he went on after waiting in vain for Ken's answer. "It won't worry anyone. They know you're ours for good, regardless of what you may think at the moment. Wait until the craving comes on—you'll see."

"How long will that be?" The point was of sufficient interest to Ken to overcome his lethargy.

"Five to six days; it varies a little with the subject. Let me warn you now—don't cross Laj Drai, ever. He really has the ship. If he keeps the tofacco from you for even half an hour after the craving comes on, you'll never forget it. I still haven't gotten over his believing that I told you where we were." Again surprise caused Ken to speak.

"You? Are you—?"

"A sniffer? Yes. They got me years ago, just like you, when I began to get an idea of what this was all about. I didn't know where this system was, but my job required me to get engineering supplies occasionally, and they didn't want me talking."

"That was why you didn't speak to me outside the observatory, just after we got back from the caves?"

"You saw me come out of the office? I never knew you were there. Yes, that was the reason, all right." Feth's normally dour features grew even grimmer at the memory. Ken went back to his own gloomy thought, which gradually crystallized into a resolve. He hesitated for a time before deciding to mention it aloud, but was unable to see what harm could result.

"Maybe you can't get out from under this stuff—I don't know; but I'll certainly try."

"Of course you will. So did I."

"Well, even if I can't Drai needn't think I'm going to

help him mass produce this hellish stuff. He can keep me under his power, but he can't compel me to think."

"He could, if he knew you weren't. Remember what I told you—not a single open act of rebellion is worth the effort. I don't know that he actually enjoys holding out on a sniffer, but he certainly never hesitates if he thinks there's need—and you're guilty until proved innocent. If I were you, I'd go right on developing those caves."

"Maybe you would. At least, I'll see to it that the caves never do him any good."

Feth was silent for a moment. If he felt any anger at the implication in Ken's statement, his voice did not betray it, however.

"That, of course, is the way to do it. I am rather surprised that you have attached no importance to the fact that Drai has made no progress exploring Planet Three for the seventeen years I have been with him."

For nearly a minute Ken stared at the mechanic, while his mental picture of the older being underwent a gradual but complete readjustment.

"No," he said at last, "I never thought of that at all. I should have, too—I did think that some of the obstacles to investigation of the planet seemed rather odd. You mean you engineered the television tube failures, and all such things?"

"The tubes, yes. That was easy enough—just make sure there were strains in the glass before the torpedo took off."

"But you weren't here when the original torpedoes were lost, were you?"

"No, that was natural enough. The radar impulses we pick up are real, too; I don't know whether this idea of a hostile race living on the blue plains of Planet Three is true or not, but there seems to be some justification for the theory. I've been tempted once or twice to put the wrong thickness of anti-radar coating on a torpedo so that they'd know we were getting in—but then I remember that that might stop the supply of tofacco entirely. Wait a few days before you think too hardly of me for that." Ken nodded slowly in understanding, then looked up suddenly as another idea struck him.

"Say, then the failure of that suit we sent to Three was not natural?"

"I'm afraid not." Feth smiled a trifle. "I overtightened the packing seals at knees, hips and handler joints while you were looking on. They contracted enough to let air out, I imagine—I haven't seen the suit, remember. I didn't want you walking around on that planet—you could do too much for this gang in an awfully short time, I imagine."

"But surely that doesn't matter now? Can't we find an excuse for repeating the test?"

"Why? I thought you weren't going to help."

"I'm not, but there's an awfully big step between getting a first hand look at the planet and taking living specimens of tofacco away from it. If you sent a person to make one landing on Sarr, what would be the chance of his landing within sight of a *Gree* bush? or, if he did, of your finding it out against his wish?"

"The first point isn't so good; this tofacco might be all over the place like *Mekko*—the difficulty would be to miss a patch of it. Your second consideration, however, now has weight." He really smiled, for the first time since Ken had known him. "I see you are a scientist after all. No narcotics agent would care in the least about the planet, under the circumstances. Well, I expect the experiment can be repeated more successfully, though I wouldn't make the dive myself for anything I can think of."

"I'll bet you would—for one thing," Ken replied. Feth's smile disappeared.

"Yes—just one," he agreed soberly. "But I see no chance of that. It would take a competent medical researcher years, even on Sarr with all his facilities. What hope would we have here?"

"I don't know, but neither of us is senile," retorted Ken. "It'll be a few years yet before I give up hope. Let's look at that suit you fixed, and the one I wore on Four. They may tell us something of what we'll have to guard against." This was the first Feth had heard of the sortie on Mars, and he said so. Ken told of his experience in detail, while the mechanic listened carefully.

"In other words," he said at the end of the tale, "there was no trouble until you actually touched this stuff you have decided was hydrogen oxide. That means it's either a terrifically good conductor, has an enormous specific heat, a large heat of vaporization, or two or three of those in combination. Right?" Ken admitted, with some surprise, that that was right. He had not summed up the matter so concisely in his own mind. Feth went on: "There is at the moment no way of telling whether there is much of that stuff on Three, but the chances are there is at least some. It follows that the principal danger on that planet seems to be encountering deposits of this chemical. I am quite certain that I can insulate a suit so that you will not suffer excessive heat loss by conduction or convection in atmospheric gases, whatever they are."

Ken did not voice his growing suspicion that Feth had been more than a mechanic in his time. He kept to the vein of the conversation.

"That seems right. I've seen the stuff, and it's certainly easy to recognize, so there should be no difficulty in avoiding it."

"You've seen the solid form, which sublimed in a near vacuum. Three has a respectable atmospheric pressure, and there may be a liquid phase of the compound. If you see any pools of any sort of liquid whatever, I would advise keeping clear of them."

"Sound enough—only, if the planet is anything like Sarr, there isn't a chance in a thousand of landing near open liquid."

"Our troubles seem to spring mostly from the fact that this planet *isn't* anything like Sarr," Feth pointed out drily. Ken was forced to admit the justice of this statement, and stored away the rapidly growing stock of information about his companion. Enough of Feth's former reserve had disappeared to make him seem a completely changed person.

The suits were brought into the shop and gone over with extreme care. The one used on Planet Four appeared to have suffered no damage, and they spent most of the time on the other. The examination this time was much more minute than the one Ken had given it on board the *Karella,* and one or two new discoveries resulted. Besides the bluish deposit Ken had noted on the metal, which he was now able to show contained oxides, there was a looser encrustation in several more protected spots which gave a definite potassium spectrum—one of the few that Ken could readily recognize—and also a distinct odor of carbon bisulfide when heated. That, to the chemist, was completely inexplicable. He was familiar with gaseous compounds of both elements, but was utterly unable to imagine how there could have been precipitated from them anything capable of remaining solid at "normal" temperature.

Naturally, he was unfamiliar with the makeup of earthly planets, and had not seen the fire whose remains had so puzzled Roger Wing. Even the best imaginations have their limits when data are lacking.

The joints had, as Feth expected, shrunk at the seals, and traces of oxides could be found in the insulation. Apparently some native atmosphere had gotten into the suit, either by diffusion or by outside pressure after the sulfur had frozen.

"Do you think that is likely to happen with the packing properly tightened?" Ken asked, when this point had been checked.

"Not unless the internal heaters fail from some other cause, and in that case you won't care anyway. The over-tightening cut down the fluid circulation in the temperature equalizing shell, so that at first severe local cooling could take place without causing a sufficiently rapid reaction in the main heaters. The local coils weren't up to the job, and once the fluid had frozen at the joints of course the rest was only a matter of seconds. I suppose we might use something with a lower freezing point than zinc as an equalizing fluid—potassium or sodium would be best from that point of view, but they're nasty liquids to handle from chemical considerations. Tin or bismuth are all right that way, but their specific heats are much lower than that of zinc. I suspect the best compromise would be selenium."

"I see you've spent a good deal of time thinking this out. What would be wrong with a low specific heat liquid?"

"It would have to be circulated much faster, and I don't know whether the pumps would handle it—both those metals are a good deal denser than zinc, too. Selenium is still pretty bad in specific heat, but its lower density will help the pumps. The only trouble is getting it. Well, it was just a thought—the zinc should stay liquid if nothing special goes wrong. We can try it on the next test, anyway."

"Have you thought about how you are going to justify this next trial, when Drai asks how come?"

"Not in detail. He won't ask. He likes to boast that he doesn't know any science—then he gloats about hiring brains when he needs them. We'll simply say that we have found a way around the cause of the first failure—which is certainly true enough."

"Could we sneak a televisor down on the next test, so we could see what goes on?"

"I don't see how we could conceal it—any signal we can receive down here can be picked up as well or better in the observatory. I suppose we might say that you had an idea in that line too, and we were testing it out."

"We could—only perhaps it would be better to separate ideas a little. It wouldn't help if Drai began to think you were a fool. People too often connect fools and knaves in figures of speech, and it would be a pity to have him thinking along those lines."

"Thanks—I was hoping you'd keep that point in mind. It doesn't matter much anyway—I don't see why we can't take the *Karella* out near Three and make the tests from there. That would take only a matter of minutes, and you could make the dive right away if things went well. I know it will be several days before the ship will be wanted—more likely several weeks. They get eight or ten loads of tofacco from the planet during the 'season' and several days elapse between each load. Since all the trading is done by torpedo, Lee has a nice idle time of it."

"That will be better. I still don't much like free fall, but a few hours of that will certainly be better than days of waiting. Go ahead and put it up to Drai. One other thing—let's bring more than one suit this time. I was a little worried for a while, there, out on Four."

"A good point. I'll check three suits, and then call Drai." Conversation lapsed, and for the next few hours a remarkable amount of constructive work was accomplished. The three units of armor received an honest preservice check this time, and Feth was no slacker. Pumps, valves, tanks, joints, heating coils—everything was tested, separately and in all combinations.

"A real outfit would spray them with liquid mercury as a final trick," Feth said as he stepped back from the last suit, "but we don't have it, and we don't have any place to try it, and it wouldn't check as cold as these are going to have to take anyway. I'll see what Drai has to say about using the ship—we certainly can't run three torpedoes at once, and I'd like to be sure all these suits are serviceable before any one of them is worn on Three." He was putting away his tools as he spoke. That accomplished, he half turned toward the communicator, then appeared to think better of it.

"I'll talk to him in person. Drai's a funny chap," he said, and left the shop.

He was back in a very few minutes, grinning.

"*We* can go," he said. "He was very particular about the plural. You haven't been through a period of tofacco-need yet, and he is afraid you'd get funny ideas alone. He is sure that I'll have you back here in time for my next dose. He didn't *say* all this, you understand, but it wasn't hard to tell what he had in mind."

"Couldn't we smuggle enough tofacco aboard to get us back to Sarr?"

"Speaking for myself, I couldn't get there. I understand you don't know the direction yourself. Furthermore, if Drai himself can't smuggle the stuff onto Sarr, how do you expect me to get it past his eyes? I can't carry a refrigerator on my back, and you know what happens if the stuff warms up."

"All right—we'll play the game as it's dealt for a while. Let's go."

Half an hour later, the *Karella* headed out into the icy dark. At about the same time, Roger Wing began to feel cold himself, and decided to give up the watch for that night. He was beginning to feel a little discouraged, and as he crawled through his bedroom window a short time later—with elaborate precautions of silence—and stowed the rope under his bed, he was wondering seriously if he should continue the vigil. Perhaps the strange visitor would never return, and the longer he waited to get his father's opinion, the harder it would be to show any concrete evidence of what had happened.

He fell asleep over the problem—somewhere about the time the test torpedo entered atmosphere a few miles above him.

13

The *Karella* hung poised deep in Earth's shadow, well beyond measurable air pressure. The spherical compass tuned to the transmitter on the planet far below pointed in a direction that would have been straight down had there been any weight. Ordon Lee was reading, with an occasional glance at his beloved indicator board whenever a light blinked. This was fairly often, for Ken and Feth had put the testing of cold-armor on a mass-production basis. One of the suits had already returned and been checked; Feth was now in the open air lock, clad in an ordinary space suit, detaching the second from the cargo rings and putting the third in its place. He was in touch with Ken, at the torpedo controls, by radio. The scientist was holding the torpedo as well as he could partly inside the lock, which had not been designed for such maneuvers and was not large enough for the full length of the projectile. Feth was having his troubles from the same fact, and the lock-obstruction light on Lee's board was flashing hysterically.

With the torpedo once more plunging toward the dark surface below, things quieted down a little—but only a little. Feth brought the second suit inside, necessarily closing the outer door in the process and occasioning another pattern of colored light to disturb the pilot's reading. Then there was nothing but the fading proximity light as the torpedo receded, and the burden of divided attention was shifted to Ken. He had to stay at his controls, but he wanted desperately to see what Feth was doing. He already knew that the first of the suits was wearable—its interior temperature had dropped about forty degrees; which represented an actual heat loss his own metabolism could easily make up; and there was a governor on the heater unit which Feth had deliberately set down so that the heat loss should be measurable. With that limitation removed, he should be as comfortable on the Planet of Ice as anyone could expect to be while encased in nearly three hundred pounds of metal.

Knowing this, he was less worried about the second suit; but he found that he was still unable to concentrate completely on the job in hand. He was quite startled when a buzzer sounded on his own board, which proved to be announcing the fact that his torpedo had encountered outside pressure. As Ken had not reduced its speed to anything like a safe value, he was quite busy for a while; and when he had finally landed the messenger—safely, he hoped—Feth had finished his work. There were now two usable suits.

That removed the greatest load from the minds of both scientist and mechanic, and they were not too disappointed when the third unit failed its test. Ken had a suspicion of the reason—Feth found that leakage had occurred at leg and "sleeve" joints, which would have been put under considerable stress by high acceleration. He did not volunteer this idea, and Feth asked no questions. Ken had an uneasy idea that the mechanic with the rather surprising chemical and physical background might have figured the matter out for himself, however.

This worry, if it could be dignified by such a name, was quickly submerged in the flurry of final preparations for the descent. Ordon Lee still refused flatly to lower his ship into the heat-trap of Earth's atmosphere, even after the success of two of the suits; it would therefore be necessary for Ken to ride down as the empty armor had done—clamped to the outside of a torpedo. The attachments would have to be modified so that he could manipulate them himself, and that took a little time. Ken ate a good meal, and took the unusual precaution of drinking—the Sarrians manufactured nearly all the liquid they needed in their own tissues.

If the scientist felt any slight doubts as he stepped into the metallic bulk which was to be his only shield for the next few hours from the ghastliest environment he could imagine, his pride prevented them from showing. He was silent as Feth carefully dogged the upper section in place—entry was effected through the top—and listened with a tiny stethoscope to each of the equalizer pumps as they were turned on. Satisfied, he nodded approval at the armored scientist, and Ken reached out, seized a stanchion with one of his handlers, and pulled his personal tank into motion toward the air lock. He had to wait in the corridor while Feth redonned his own suit, and then patiently inside the lock while the mechanic carefully attached the armor to the hull of the torpedo. Lee had finally become helpful, and was holding the projectile inside the lock against the pull of the meteor repellers, which he still refused to turn off for an instant.

Even when the outer door closed between Ken and the rest of the livable space within several million miles, he managed to keep his self control. He was now used to weightlessness, fortunately; the endless-fall sensation has serious mental effects on some people. Even the relative emptiness of the surrounding space he could stand, since he could see enough objects to keep himself oriented. There were about as many stars visible here as near his home planet, since two hundred parsecs mean little in the size of the galaxy.

In fact, he retained his calm until his eyes as well as his sense of balance agreed to tell him he was falling. The *Karella* had long since vanished behind—or above—him. The sun was in almost the same direction, since there had been no discussion needed to settle that the landing should be made on the day side of the planet. Rather more had been needed before the same old landing place had been selected—Ken, of course, wanted to see the natives, but even his scientific curiosity had been tempered with caution. Feth, regarding the trip chiefly as another test of the armor, had been rather against natives as an added complication; but curiosity had won out. Ken was falling toward the homing transmitter at which the trading was done, with the understanding that he would be carried a little to the west, as before—he was willing to meet "his" native, but did not want to interfere more than necessary with trade. He realized, of course, that the creatures probably moved around, but he resolutely declined to think about the probable results if the one he had frightened had met the traders; he regarded it as profitless guesswork, which it certainly would have been.

The result of all the discussion, however, meant that he could see clearly the expanding world below—it felt like below, since Feth was now slowing the torpedo's descent. He could not see the torpedo at all easily, as his armor was facing away from it and the back view ports in the helmet were too close to the hull for real vision. He was beginning to feel, therefore, like a man hanging from the ledge of a high roof on a rope of questionable strength. If his vocal apparatus had been as closely connected with his breathing mechanism as is that of a human being, his state of mind would certainly have been betrayed by the radio to the listeners above. As it was they could not hear his tense breathing, and he endured his terror in silence and alone. It was probably just as well; Ordon Lee's reaction would hardly have been a sympathetic one, and whatever helpful feeling Feth might have had he would have been likely to express aloud.

There was air around him now—at least the gaseous mixture this world used for air. It was whistling upward, audible even through the armor. He could not be much more than five miles from the ground, and the descent was still rapid—too rapid, he was beginning to feel. As if in answer to the thought, his weight increased abruptly, and he knew that Feth far above had added power. With an effort greater than he had thought himself capable of making, Ken wrenched his attention from the rapid expansion of the landscape below and the creaking of the taut chains above, and concentrated on details. Once started, this proved easy, for there was more that was fantastic around him than mere temperature.

He could not see too far, of course. Eyes whose greatest sensitivity lies in the blue and near ultra-violet work are at a considerable disadvantage in Earth's hazy atmosphere. Still, the ground below was taking on detail.

It was rough, as they had deduced. Even though mountains do not show to best advantage from overhead, Ken was experienced enough to judge that these were quite respectable heights by Sarrian standards. The surface was buried in a riot of color, largely varying shades of green, brown, and gray. Here and there a patch of metallic sheen reminded him disquietingly of the vast, smooth areas where the mysteriously hostile intelligences of the planet dwelt. If these were outposts—but they had never interfered with the trading torpedoes which had been descending for years in this same area, Ken told himself.

As he dropped lower, he saw that some of the gray elevations were of remarkable shape and form—many of them were actually broader above than lower down. He was quite low before he could see that these objects were not part of the landscape, but were actually suspended in the air. The only clouds he had ever seen were the vast dust storms raised by Sarr's furious winds, but he judged that these must be of somewhat similar nature. Probably the particles were smaller, to permit them to remain in suspension—a planet this cold could hardly have very strong winds. He described the phenomena as minutely as he could to the listeners above. Feth reported that he was putting Ken's broadcasts on record, and added some more pertinent information.

"Your descent has been almost stopped, now. You are about one mile above the transmitter, and a few hundred feet higher above the place where the atmosphere tests were made. Do you want to go straight down now, or stay there and observe for a while?"

"Down with moderate speed, please. It is not possible to see too far, and I'd like to get down to where real details are visible. It seems to be mountainous country—I'll try to guide you in landing me near some peak, so that I can observe for a reasonable distance from a stable spot."

"All right. You're going down." Two or three minutes passed silently; then Ken spoke again.

"Are you moving me horizontally?"

"No. You are already away from over the transmitter—three or four miles."

"Then this atmosphere has stronger currents than I expected. I am drifting visibly, though not rapidly. It's rather hard to specify the direction—the sun is not very far from straight up, and the torpedo hides it."

"When you're nearly down, give me the direction with respect to the torpedo's orientation. I'll stop you before you touch."

Gradually details grew clearer. The greenness seemed

to be a tangled mass of material somewhat resembling chemical growths Ken had prepared in various solutions; he tentatively identified it as plant life, and began to suspect what had caused the crackling sound when the test torpedo had been landed.

Standing out from the green were areas quite obviously of bare rock. These seemed to be located for the most part at and near the tops of the mountains; and with infinite care Ken directed his distant pilot in an approach to one of these. Finally, hanging motionless twenty feet above a surface which even in this relatively dim light was recognizable as rock, he gave the order to lower away.

Six feet from the ground, he had the machine stopped again, and carefully released the leg chains. The lower part of his armor dropped, almost touching; a word into the microphone brought the metal feet into contact with the ground. Releasing one of the upper chains caused him to swing around, still leaning at a sharp angle with one side up toward the supporting hull. By a species of contortionism he contrived to make a workable tripod of his legs and the rear prop of the armor, and at last released the final chain. He was standing on the Planet of Ice, on his own two feet.

He felt heavy, but not unbearably so. His extreme caution not to land in a recumbent position was probably well founded—it was very unlikely that he could have raised himself and the armor to a standing posture with his own muscles in this gravity. Walking was going to be difficult, too—possibly even dangerous; the rock was far from level.

This, of course, was not the principal matter. For several minutes after he had severed connections with the torpedo, Ken made no attempt to move; he simply stood where he was, listening to the almost inaudible hum of his circulation motors and wondering when his feet would start to freeze. Nothing seemed to happen, however, and presently he began to take a few cautious steps. The joints of his armor were still movable; evidently the zinc had not yet frozen.

The torpedo had drifted away from overhead; apparently a slight wind was blowing. At Ken's advice, Feth brought the machine to the ground. Even with his fear lost in curiosity, Ken had no intention of becoming separated by any great distance from his transportation. Once assured that it was remaining in place, he set to work.

A few minutes' search located several loose rock fragments. These he picked up and placed in the torpedo, since anything might be of some interest; but he principally wanted soil—soil in which things were visibly growing. Several times he examined rock specimens as closely as he could, hoping to find something that might resemble the minute plants of Planet Four; but he failed utterly to recognize as life the gray and black crustose lichens which were actually growing on some of the fragments.

The landscape was not barren, however. Starting a few hundred yards from his point of landing, and appearing with ever-increasing frequency as one proceeded down the mountainside, there were bushes and patches of moss which gradually gave way to dwarfed trees and finally, where the rock disappeared for good beneath the soil, to full grown firs. Ken saw this, and promptly headed for the nearest clump of bushes. As an afterthought, he told Feth what he was doing, so that the torpedo could be sent along. There was no point, he told himself, in carrying all the specimens back up the hillside.

Progress was quite difficult, since a gap a foot wide between rocks presented a major obstacle to the armor. After a few minutes of shuffling punctuated with frequent pauses for rest, he remarked:

"The next time, we'd better have longer shoulder chains. Then I can hang right side up from the torpedo, and be spared all this waddling."

"That's a thought," replied Feth. "It certainly will be easy enough. Do you want to come back up now and make the change, or collect a few things first?"

"Oh, I'll stay a while, now that I'm here. I haven't

much farther to travel to get to these plants, if they are plants. The darned things are green, at least partly. I suppose, though, that objectively speaking there should be nothing surprising about that. Well, here we go again."

He lifted his prop from the ground and shuffled forward once more. Another minute or two sufficed to bring him within reach of the strange growth. It was only about a foot high, and he was even less able to bend down to it than he had been on Planet Four; so he extended a handler to seize a branch. The results were a trifle startling.

The branch came away easily enough. There was no trouble about that. However, before he had time to raise it to his eyes a puff of smoke spurted from the point where the handler was touching it, and the tissue in the immediate neighborhood of the metal began to turn black. The memories aroused by this phenomenon caused Ken to drop the branch, and he would undoubtedly have taken a step backward had the armor been less cumbersome. As it was, he remembered almost instantly that no gas could penetrate his metal defenses, and once more picked up the bit of vegetation.

The smoke reappeared and grew thicker as he lifted it toward his face port, but he had several seconds to examine its structure before the smoldering wood burst into flame. Although this startled him almost as much as the earlier phenomenon had, he retained his hold on the fragment. He watched with interest as the main branch curled, blackened, glowed, and flamed away, the drier leaves following suit while the green ones merely browned slightly. He made an effort to capture some of the traces of ash that remained when the process was completed, but all he was able to save were some bits of charcoal from the less completely burned portions. This he also stowed in the torpedo, Feth guiding the little vessel over to him in response to spoken directions.

A bit of soil, scraped up from beneath the plant,

smoked but did not burn. Ken obtained a number of airtight cans from the cargo compartment of the torpedo and spent some time scooping bits of soil up in these. He also compressed some of the air into a cylinder, using a small piston-type pump from which Feth had carefully removed all traces of lubricant. It leaked a trifle, but its moving parts moved, which was a pleasant surprise.

"There," said Ken, when the task was completed. "If there are any seeds in that earth, we should be able to build a little vivarium and find out at least something about this life and its needs."

"Do you have a balance between makers and eaters?" asked Feth. "Suppose these plants are all—what would you call them? oxidizers?—and you don't have the corresponding reducers. I should think you'd need a balance of some sort, with any sort of life—otherwise you'd have perpetual motion."

"I can't tell that, of course, until we try. Still, I might go down this mountain a little farther and try to pick up a wider variety. There are still some empty cans."

"Another point—I don't recall your making any arrangement to keep them at the proper temperature. I know they're almost as cold as outer space, but there's a difference between almost and all the way."

"We'll leave the cans in the torpedo until we get back to One. With no air, they'll change temperature very slowly, and we can leave the torpedo somewhere on the twilight zone of One where it'll stay about the right temperature until we can build a chamber with thermostats and a refrigerator—it won't be very large; I have only a couple of cubic yards of air."

"All right, I guess you win. If it doesn't work, it will be small loss anyway. Are your feet getting cold yet?"

"Not so far—and believe me, I'm looking for it!"

"I'm not sure I believe you. I have a pretty good idea of where most of your attention is. Have you seen any animal life? I've heard the old buzzing once or twice."

"Have you? I hadn't noticed it. All I can hear comes

from the mike in the torpedo, so I should get anything you do."

"I told you where your attention was. Well, I'll call you if I hear it again." He fell silent, and Ken resumed his laborious journey downhill. With frequent rests, he finally succeeded in filling and sealing all his containers and depositing them in the cargo space of the torpedo. He was interrupted once by Feth, who reported that the buzzing was again audible; but even though Ken himself could hear it when he listened, he was unable to find the source. Flies are not very large creatures, and the light was very dim anyway by Sarrian standards. Since there was nothing very appetizing even for a fly in the cargo compartment above which the microphone was located, the buzzing presently ceased.

Ken took a final look at the landscape, describing everything as completely as he could so that the record being made far above would be useful. The peaks stood out far more prominently now, since some of them were higher than he was. By ignoring the vegetation with which their slopes were clothed and imagining that it was sunset just after a particularly good dust storm, he was even able to find something almost homelike in the scene—there were times when even Sarr's blue-white sun could look as dull as the luminary of this icy world. At such times, of course, there was always a wind which would put Earth's wildest hurricane to shame, and the silence around him was out of place on that score; but for just a moment his imagination was able to carry him across two hundred parsecs of emptiness to a world of warmth and life.

He came to himself with a little start. This place was nothing like home—it wasn't exactly dead, but it should be; dead as the vacuum of space it so greatly resembled. Its cold was beginning to creep into him, mentally in the form of a return of the horror he had felt the first time he had seen the planet and physically by a slight ache in his feet. Even the engineering miracle he was wearing could not keep out the fingers of the cold indefinitely. He started to call Feth, to have the torpedo lifted so that he could get at the chains and clamps; but the request was not uttered.

As suddenly as it had done a few days before, a human voice cut sharply through the stillness of the Planet of Ice.

14

It was not, in the end, his own discouragement which caused the cessation of Roger's nocturnal watchings. The night on which the Sarrians tested the armor was, indeed, the last of these journeys; but this was owing to reasons beyond the boy's control. When he descended in the morning, his father met him and accompanied him outside. There he pointed out certain footprints. Then they went up to Roger's room together, and the rope came to light. Mr. Wing concluded the proceedings with a request for an explanation.

"Don't get the idea that anyone tattled," he added. "I don't know whether you have anyone in your confidence, even. Both your mother and I saw that you were getting most of your sleep done daytimes. Well, what's the story?"

Roger never even thought of lying. The family custom of proving questionable statements on challenge had taught him, as it had the other children, to recognize evidence and forego useless denial. The only question in his mind was whether to tell or not. He knew there would be no punishment if he refused; but also, there would be no help from his father on a problem that was decidedly beyond his own abilities, and there would most certainly be no more night journeys in search of landing torpedoes. He told what had happened, with all the detail the near-eidetic memory of childhood could evoke. His father was silent for a minute or two when he had finished.

"We'll say nothing about your following Don and me," he said at last. "You were never told in so many words not to, and curiosity is a healthy trait. Of course you let yourself get caught in the woods at night without food, water or light, and that is a more serious matter in view of the fact that you're supposed to know better. However, the story being as interesting as it is, I guess we'll suspend sentence on that offense." Roger grinned.

"What would the sentence have been?"

"The logical one would be restriction to the half-mile circle for a week or two. You certainly behaved like a six-year-old. Let's consider that that's hanging over your head, and go on to more immediate matters. I suppose Edie knows all about this?"

"She knows about what happened that night. Not about the times I've gone out since."

"All right. After breakfast, get her and come with me. We have a number of things to talk over."

It turned out that Don was also at the meeting. This was held in a little natural amphitheater a few yards uphill from the house, which had been fitted with split-log benches. Mr. Wing wasted no time, but told the younger children the same story he had told Donald a few days before. Then Roger repeated his tale, mostly for his older brother's benefit. Don had, of course, seen a Sarrian torpedo by this time, as he had been present when the first load of tobacco had been delivered a few days before; and there seemed to be little doubt that the structure Roger had encountered was of the same origin.

"I don't understand why they're shifting their base of operations after all these years." Mr. Wing looked puzzled. "They've been coming back to that same gadget which we think is a directional transmitter every summer since before Don was born."

"You don't really know that they haven't landed anywhere else, though," pointed out Donald. "It just happened that Roger met one of their torpedoes. There might have been any number of others, anywhere on the earth."

"That's true, of course. Rog, you didn't find any traces of other landings on these night walks of yours, did you?"

"I'm not sure, Dad. There's a little patch of bushes all by itself on a hilltop out that way, that's been burnt over. I couldn't find any sign of a campfire, and there haven't been any thunderstorms. I thought maybe one of the things had dropped something like the thing that burned my hand, and started the fire; but I couldn't find anything of the sort. I don't really know what started it."

"I see. Then to sum up, we've been trading with creatures not native to this world for a long time; we may or may not be the only ones doing so; on at least one occasion they sent down a craft whose primary mission does not seem to have been trade."

"Unless the light that Rog saw was intended to attract attention, as it did," cut in Donald.

"In that case they would hardly have had their gold too hot to be touched. Furthermore, I've always refused gold—regular prospectors are competition enough without starting a rush of amateurs."

"We don't know that other people, if there have been any, felt the same way. But I guess you're right about the temperature. They must have been conducting an experiment of their own, and the offer to trade was an afterthought when they heard Rog's voice."

"It was a dirty trick," commented Roger.

"It may have been unintentional. Their knowledge of our language is extremely limited, and apparently they can't see down here. Either they don't know about television or can't mount a transmitter in those torpedoes. Besides, if you came on them unexpectedly, they may have forgotten in the excitement of the moment that the gold would be hot. You said it was another container which was providing the light. However, that's a point there's not much use discussing.

"I had not planned to take this step until both Roger and Edie were older, and had had training enough to be of more help; but the matter seems to have been taken out of my control in that respect. What I want to do, and will need the help of all of you in doing, is to find out where these things are from, what sort of people are running them—and, if possible, how they work. I don't have to tell you how important that knowledge would be. I have never tried to get outside experts on the job, because, as I told Don, I was afraid they'd let curiosity overcome prudence. I don't want the torpedoes scared away by any hasty action. I'm too old to learn a new trade, for one thing."

"Nuts!" It was Edie's first contribution to the discussion, though she had listened intently to all that had gone before.

"What are we going to do?" Roger asked, rather more practically.

"First of all, you two will come with us the next time we trade. I may take the younger kids along too, only it's quite a walk for them. You can listen in, watch, and generally see the whole thing for yourselves. After that, ideas will be in order. I was hoping, Rog, that you'd be an electronics expert by the time this happened. However, we'll use what we have."

"Maybe my trouble the other night could be put to use," Roger suggested. "If they want tobacco badly enough to pay for it in platinum and iridium, they might be in a mood to apologize."

"Supposing they realize they hurt you, and could think of a way to transmit the apology. I won't refuse an extra nugget or two if they choose to send them, but that won't be very informative."

"I suppose that's so. Well, anyway, I'm going to go over the whole neighborhood of where I saw it and where you do your trading, by daylight. If they've made any other landings in the woods, I'll find 'em—that one broke a lot of branches, and left a dent in the ground the shape of the torpedo."

"If you think it's worth doing," remarked Don. "Why should they have landed in this neighborhood? Earth's a pretty big place."

"They did once, and I bet I know why!" retorted Roger. "That transmitter is right here! If you were exploring a new world or a new country even, would you make one landing here and another five hundred miles away? You would not. You'd get to know one neighborhood first, and plant an outpost, and then spread out from there."

There was silence for two or three minutes while the others absorbed this.

"You're assuming, then," said Mr. Wing at last, "that after twenty years of mere trading, they suddenly are starting to explore? Why didn't they do it sooner?"

"Unfair question."

"True enough. All right, it's certainly a usable working hypothesis. You may go ahead with your exploring—so may Edie if she wants. I'm not sold enough on your idea to spend the effort myself, but in a day or two I'll signal for another torpedo. That will give you time to do any looking you want, I suppose?"

"Well—" Roger's recent mapping activities had given him a much clearer idea than he had formerly held just what the examining of one square mile meant. "We can look around a bit, anyway. I'm going right now, if no one has any real ideas. Coming, Edie?" The girl stood up silently, and followed him back to the house. Their father watched them go with some amusement.

"I wish I didn't have a nagging worry about Rog's theory," he said suddenly to Donald. "He might just be right—these creatures might be tired of paying for tobacco and they certainly know more of physical science than we do."

"They'll have a fine time looking for the living weed in this neighborhood," replied his son. "They'll do better to stay on peaceful terms."

"Just tell 'em that, will you?" murmured Mr. Wing.

Roger and his sister wasted no time. This time there was no mistake in the matter of food; they hastily prepared some sandwiches—their mother had long since resigned herself to the fact that raids on the pantry were inseparable from common-sense rules of forest life—and with a canteen of water apiece they set out eastward. Billy and Marge were playing somewhere out of sight, so there was no trouble about leaving them home. Their father's description had been clear enough so that they had no trouble in finding the Sarrian transmitter, and from there the two began their search. At Edie's suggestion they split up, she taking the southern slopes on the line back to their home and Roger taking the northern. They agreed to keep to high ground as much as possible, and thus remain in earshot of each other most of the time. There was little point, in the time available, to look for traces in the woods; but it might be possible to sight either burned spots such as Roger had already seen or traces of disturbance in the upper branches of trees while looking from above. At any rate, more territory could be examined. Neither youngster had spent any time debating the question of whether it was better to know about a small area or guess about a large one.

Neither Roger nor Edith was on the hill where Ken landed at the time of his descent. Nature had arranged that they should be in the neighborhood, but coincidence refused to carry matters farther. However, Nature still had a trick in reserve.

Roger, until that morning, had taken more or less for granted that any future visits of the torpedo would be at night, as the first had been. His father's story had changed that idea; and since he had heard it only three or four hours before, he had not given up taking rather frequent looks at the sky. It was not too surprising, therefore, that he saw the descending torpedo.

It was nearly a mile and a half away, and he could make out no details; but he was certain it was no bird. The irregularity caused by Ken's dangling form gave just a suggestion of oddness at that distance. Detailed or not, however, Roger never thought of doubting what it was; and with a whoop that might or might not reach his sister's ears for all he cared at the moment, he headed downhill at a breakneck pace.

For a short time he made excellent speed, the irregularity of the rocks offering no obstacle that his alert eyes and active muscles could not overcome without trouble. Then he reached the forest, and was slowed considerably. For a short distance he kept up the furious effort with which he had started; then realizing that he had at least one hill to cross and another to climb, he eased off a little.

He had wet feet, thoroughly scratched legs, and a decided shortness of wind when he reached the hilltop toward which the torpedo had seemed to be descending, some three quarters of an hour later. He had seen no sign of Edith—he had, in fact, completely forgotten her. She might have come back to mind as he paused at the top of the small mountain to gain his breath and look around for the object of his search; but as it happened, the torpedo was in sight, only a short distance down the other side. So was Sallman Ken.

Roger had seen pictures of the tremendous pressure suits which have from time to time been constructed for deep-sea exploration. The sight of Ken, therefore, did not astonish him too much—certainly less than the sight of a Sarrian without armor would have done. The suit the scientist was wearing humanized his appearance considerably, since a human being would not have had to be too greatly distorted to get into it.

The legs, for engineering reasons, had only a single "knee," corresponding to the upper joint of the Sarrian limb; the body was about human size, and cylindrical in shape; there were only two upper limbs. These were more flexible than a human being would have needed in a similar suit, but they at least gave no indication that the creature wearing them was controlling them with two tentacles each. The handlers at their extremities were natural enough, though more complicated than the claw-like devices the boy had seen in the diving suit pictures.

At his distance, he could not see clearly through the transparent ports in the helmet; and so for some moments he failed to realize just how unhuman the wearer of the clumsy garment was.

For perhaps half a minute, Roger simply stared; then he unloosed the yell which interrupted Ken's "embarkation." The scientist's attention had been completely taken up with this task, and he had not seen Roger at all before the cry; after it, he saw nothing else. He himself was not facing the direction from which the sound had come, but one of the transparent ports in his helmet was; and he was much too interested to devote attention to anything like turning the armor, after his first look at the being charging downhill toward him. He simply stood, watching with the one eye he could bring to bear. It never occurred to him for an instant that the creature might be hostile.

Roger never thought of the possibility either. His mind resembled that of Ken much too closely, in spite of the overwhelming physical differences. They simply stood facing each other—Ken finally did swing his armor around, so he could use both eyes—and silently absorbed all the details their respective optics could pick out. Each had an advantage—Roger in the fact that the light was normal for him, Ken in that the boy was not concealed in a couple of hundred pounds of metal. Roger could see the Sarrian's face now, and his attention was taken up completely with the great, widespread, independently movable eyes, the blank where a nose should have been, and the broad, thin-lipped, surprisingly human mouth. The silence stretched out.

It was interrupted by Feth, whose anxiety had been increasing with each second that passed after Roger's call.

"What's happened? Is anything wrong? Are you all right, Ken?" The scientist found his voice.

"Perfectly all right. We have company, as I suppose you guessed." He began to describe Roger as completely as possible, and was interrupted within a minute by the mechanic.

"It can't be done. We'll get a television set or a camera down there if I have to invent a whole new system. Never mind describing the thing—see if you can talk to it!"

Roger had heard none of this, since Feth had not energized the speaker in the torpedo. This oversight he now rectified, and Ken's next words reached the boy clearly.

"What in the Galaxy can I say? Suppose this one has heard about our mistake the other night—suppose it's even the same one? If I use the word 'Gold' it'll either run or start fighting. I'm not afraid of it, but that certainly wouldn't help the process of getting acquainted."

"Well, you've just used the word. How did he take it? I have the main speaker on." Ken, who had had no means of knowing that fact, cast a startled glance at Roger.

The boy, of course, had understood just the one word "Gold." He probably would have missed that, except for the fact that Ken had accentuated it as one does a foreign word; but as it was, he thought that the previous conversation had been addressed to him. He had not distinguished the two voices, and all the sounds had come from the torpedo still poised just above Ken's head.

"I don't want any of your gold—not if it's like the last batch!" Again only one word was understood by the listener. Ken grew hopeful. Maybe this creature hadn't heard, or maybe they had completely misinterpreted the sounds he and Feth had heard during the atmosphere test.

"Gold?" he asked.

"NO!" Roger shook his head negatively and backed away as he gave the emphatic answer. The first gesture meant nothing to the watching Sarrian, but the second seemed clear enough.

"Did you get that last sound of his on record, Feth? Judging by his actions, that's the negative in their language. No gold!" he addressed the last two words after a brief pause. Roger relaxed visibly, but still spoke emphatically.

"No gold, no platinum,—I have no tobacco." He spread empty hands and turned out his pockets, giving the Sarrian scientist a clue he had been waiting for on just how much of his covering was artificial.

"Point to things and name them!" Feth cut in from above. "How else can you learn a language? This chatter sounds as silly as anything I've ever heard!"

"All right—only remember, I can see as well as hear. That makes a bit of difference. If you expect any results, keep quiet; how's this thing going to tell who's talking? It all comes from the same loudspeaker. I'll call you when I want to hear from you." Feth gave no answer to this very sound point, and after waiting a minute Ken began to follow the mechanic's suggestion.

Since Roger had been thinking of exactly the same thing, he caught on at once, and thereby gave the Sarrian a higher opinion of human intelligence than his conversations with Laj Drai had caused him to hold previously. The English words for rock, tree, bush, mountain, cloud, and the numbers up to ten were learned in short order. A few verbs were managed easily enough. At this point operations seemed likely to be suspended, and Roger was rather relieved to have the subject changed by a distant hail.

"My gosh! I forgot all about Edie! She must think I fell off a cliff or something!" He turned in the direction from which the faint voice seemed to be coming, and put all the strength of his lungs into an answering hail. His sister heard it and responded; and ten or fifteen minutes of lung strain brought her to the scene. She seemed a little dubious about approaching Ken at all closely, to Roger's surprise.

"What's the matter with you? He just wants to talk, as far as I can see."

"Haven't you got burned again?"

"No; why should I?"

"Can't you feel the heat?"

Oddly enough, Roger hadn't. He had never come closer than about fifteen feet to the scientist. The radiation from the armor was easily detectable at that distance without being uncomfortable, but he simply had not noticed it in the press of other interests. For Edith, whose strongest impression of the aliens had been derived from her brother's experience of a few nights before, it was the most prominent characteristic of the thing standing before them.

With the matter brought to his notice, Roger approached the alien more closely, and extended a cautious hand toward the metal. He stopped it more than a foot away.

"My gosh, he certainly *is* hot. Maybe that's what caused the trouble—they never thought the gold would burn me. Do you suppose that's it?"

"Maybe. I'd like to know how it can live when it's that hot, though. So would Dad. He ought to be here anyway. Had I better go tell him, while you keep the thing here?"

"I don't know how I'd keep it. Besides, it would be awful late by the time he got here. Let's try to make a date for tomorrow." He turned back to Ken without waiting for Edie's rather sensible question, "How?"

Actually the "how" proved not too difficult. Time is an abstract quantity, but when it is measured by phenomena like the apparent movement of the sun it can be discussed in signs quite clearly enough for practical purposes. Ken understood without difficulty by the time Roger had finished waving his arms that the two natives would return to the present location shortly after sunrise the following day. The scientist was just as glad to break off the interview, since his feet were now quite numb with cold. He resumed the task of fastening himself to the hovering torpedo, and the children, turning back for a last look as they reached the trees, saw the odd-looking assemblage of suit and carrier drifting upward with ever-increasing velocity. They watched until it had dwindled to a speck and vanished; then with one accord they headed for home.

15

Mr. Wing was not merely interested; he was enthralled by the youngster's report. He was sensible enough to realize that nothing any of his family had done could possibly be responsible for the aliens' starting to make personal exploration of the earth, but the fact that they were doing so seemed likely to be very helpful to his plans. The evening meal consisted very largely of conversation, for all attempts to keep the details from any of the family were abandoned. Mrs. Wing, of course, had known everything from the beginning; Roger and Edie had been pretty well briefed that morning; but Billy and Marge lacked both specific information and basic knowledge to appreciate the situation. Their questions tended to break up the general train of thought, but only Roger showed any impatience. Since even he did not dare become openly contemptuous of their ignorance, the general tone of the conversation remained peaceful, and several important decisions were made.

"It seems to me," Mr. Wing said, "that these things—maybe we can think of them as people, now that we have some idea what they look like—must at last have some scientists on the job. I can't even guess at the reason for the delay—"

"Look at an astronomical photo of the Milky Way some time, and you might guess," cut in Don.

"Reason or no reason, the fact itself may be useful. There will be both explorers and apparatus coming down, beyond reasonable doubt; and they must expect to lose a certain amount of the latter. I don't mean to encourage dishonesty in my offspring, but if we could acquire some of that apparatus long enough to perform dissection I would be very pleased."

"I take it you are no longer afraid of scaring them off?" Mrs. Wing stated rather than asked.

"No. Whether they continue trading or not is out of my hands—it will probably depend on the results that their scientists get. I am not worried; they obviously want tobacco badly, and I doubt very much if it grows on any other planet. I could be surer of my ground, of course, if I knew what they wanted it for. I used to think they smoked it as we do, but this knowledge of their normal temperature makes that sound a trifle un-likely.

"But back to the original point. Anyone who talks to them from now on might well suggest that another transmitter be brought down, so they can home on this house. I see no point in walking five or six miles out and the same distance back just for a daily conversation. Incidentally, Rog, I'm wondering whether we mightn't have made a better impression if we'd tried learning their words for things instead of teaching them ours."

"Maybe. I didn't think of that."

"How about the trading, Dad?" asked Don. "Are you going to keep it up as usual, or try to get these investigators to take our stuff?" His father considered for a moment.

"I think we'd better stick to the old routine," he said finally. "We have no assurance that the traders and scientists are in with each other, and it would be a pity to disappoint our customers. Perhaps, when we go to keep this date tomorrow, you'd better go on to the transmitter and give the signal. You'd better carry a pack of cigarettes with you; normally, of course, they're two or three days answering, but if they should be in with the science crowd they may be a lot closer at the moment. You'd better be prepared, in case they answer at once."

"You mean I'd better stay by the transmitter all day, if necessary?"

"Well—no, not that. Hang around for a while, and then come back to where we'll be. We can keep an eye in the right direction in case another torpedo comes down—it can't be more than a couple of miles in a straight line, so we stand a fair chance of seeing it."

"All right. I signal, and everybody talks, with emphasis on suggesting that another communicator be brought down—always supposing either party learns enough of the other's language to get any such idea across." Don shifted the subject suddenly. "Say, Dad, I just had an idea. You say it doesn't always take the same length of time between the signal and the arrival of the torpedo?"

"That's right. Never less than two days, never much more than three."

"Could you give me any specific signalling dates, with the time of arrival? The more the better. I think I can do something with them." Mr. Wing thought for a moment.

"Some, anyway. I can remember those of the last couple of years pretty well, and probably some odd ones from earlier years if I try. What's your idea?"

"I'd rather not tell until I'm a little more certain of it. Let's have what you can recall."

With the aid of the family, who were able to supply clues on his dates of absence—a diary kept by Edie was very helpful—about two dozen of the dates were fixed with sufficient accuracy to satisfy Don. He immediately went up to his room, carrying the notes he had taken.

From that point the conversation drifted by imperceptible degrees into pure fantasy, and by bed-time a number of wonderful pictures had been drawn about the home life of the fiery visitors. Little Margie's was the most interesting, if the least accurate.

Sallman Ken, however, was wasting no time on fantasy. He had not yet worked out a really detailed course of action, but certain ideas were gradually taking shape in his mind as he worked.

The moment he entered the *Karella* and had emerged

from his bulky armor, he went into a close conference with Feth. Lee was present at first, even following them to Ken's quarters where the scientist began; but a glance of understanding passed between Ken and Feth, and the conversation took a remarkably abstruse turn. It had just enough meaning to give the impression that matters of highly advanced physics and chemistry were being covered, in connection with the problem of keeping the seeds—if any—in the soil samples alive and healthy. For a few minutes it looked as though Lee were going to stay and take it, but Feth suddenly had the inspiration to ask the pilot's opinion of occasional matters. After a little of this, Ordon Lee drifted back to his control room. "He's not stupid," Feth said, looking after his retreating form, "but he certainly lacks confidence in his education! Now, what did you want to keep from Drai?"

"It has occurred to me," Ken said, "that our employer is going to want to hear everything that goes on on Planet Three, as soon as we are in halfway decent communication with the natives. I have some vague ideas about the uses to which those creatures can be put, and I'd rather not have Drai listening in to all our conversations. Since at the moment there's no way of preventing that, I'd like to know whether it might not be possible to connect me up with the speaker on the torpedo *without* having everything audible up here as well. It would be best, I suppose, if I could turn your contact on and off at will, so that he'll hear enough to keep him from getting suspicious."

"I suppose it could be done, all right," the mechanic said slowly. "I'm afraid it would take more work than it's worth, though. Wouldn't it be a great deal simpler to take another set down with you in the torpedo? You already have means for tuning both transmitter and receiver in the armor, so you could switch from one set to the other whenever you pleased."

"Wouldn't they miss the extra set?"

"Not unless Drai starts paying a great deal more attention to the technical supplies than he has in the past."

"All right, let's do it that way. Now, let's see. I already suggested suspending the armor vertically instead of horizontally from the torpedo, so I can be carried around instead of having to lug that hardware against extra gravity, didn't I?"

"Yes. That will be easy enough."

"It will have another good point, as well. The only discomfort I've felt so far on that planet has been in my feet, in spite of what we feared. This way we can keep them off the ground, so they don't lose so much by conduction.

"The only other thing I had in mind had to do with torpedo control. Could a unit be made small enough for me to carry, so I could move myself around down there instead of having to tell you where I want to go?"

Feth frowned at this suggestion. "I thought of that, too, while I was trying to keep the torpedo near you this time," he said. "Frankly, I doubt it—not that the set could be made small enough, but that I could do it with the materials I have at hand. Still, I'll look into the possibility when we get back to One. I take it you have no objection to Drai's hearing about these last two suggestions?"

"Of course not. They ought to keep him happy. I suppose it would be too much to hope that he'd take a trip down there himself, once we showed it was safe enough?" Feth smiled broadly at the scientist's suggestion.

"It would take a better psychologist than either of us to endue him with that much trust in his fellows, I fear. Besides, what good would it do? We wouldn't gain anything by leaving him there, pleasant as the idea sounds, and there'd be no use trying to threaten him, since he'd never dream of keeping any inconvenient promises you might wring out of him."

"I didn't really expect much from the idea. Well, with the other matter understood, I suppose we'd better take those samples back to One before they freeze, and get a vivarium knocked together. If we can grow anything at all, it ought to keep Drai quiet for a little while."

The torpedo which had transported Ken and his specimens had been allowed to drift to the edge of the repeller field as soon as he had detached himself from it. Feth now returned to the control room and began to monitor the little vessel, holding it close against the hull of the large ship so that it would be dragged along in the *Karella*'s drive fields; and Lee, at Ken's request, headed sunward once more. A thousand miles from the surface of Mercury the torpedo was cast loose again, and Feth eased it down to a landing near the caves—a televisor had been set up there some time since, and he was able to guide the landing with the aid of this. He arranged matters so that about three feet of the torpedo's nose was in sunlight, while the rest was in the shadow of a large mass of rock. That, he judged, should maintain somewhere near the right temperature for a few hours at least.

As soon as the *Karella* was grounded, he and Ken adjourned at once to the shop. There, a metal case about a yard square and two feet high was quickly assembled. Feth very carefully welded all seams and tested them against full atmospheric pressure. A glass top was provided, sealed in place with a silicone vacuum wax that was standard equipment on any space ship; this also checked out against a pressure equivalent to an earthly barometric reading of twelve hundred fifty millimeters of mercury. A second, similar case large enough to enclose the first was under construction when Drai appeared. He had evidently noticed at last that the ship was back.

"Well, I understand from Lee that you actually talked to a native. Good work, good work. Did you find out anything about how they make their tofacco?"

"We haven't learned their language too well, yet," Feth replied with as little sarcasm as he could manage. "We were operating on a slightly different line of investigation." He indicated the partly constructed vivarium. Drai frowned at it, as though trying to gather its purpose. "It's a small chamber where we can reproduce Planet Three's conditions, we hope; more or less of an experiment. The larger one goes outside, and we'll maintain a vacuum between the two. Feth says one of the sulfur hexafluoride refrigerators he knocked together years ago will get the temperature low enough, and we got enough of the planet's air to fill it a couple of times at their pressure." Drai looked puzzled still.

"But isn't it a little small for one of the natives? Lee said you'd described them as nearly five feet tall. Besides, I didn't hear about these plans at all."

"Natives? I thought you wanted us to grow vegetation. What good would a native do us here?" The master's face cleared.

"Oh, I see. I didn't know you'd picked up vegetation already. Still, now that I think of it, it mightn't be a bad idea to have a native or two. If the race is at all civilized, they could be used for a really stupendous ransom in tofacco—and we could use them in the cave, once it was conditioned, to take care of the tofacco and harvest it. Thanks for the idea."

"I don't know just how intelligent the natives are, as yet," replied Ken, "but I don't think they're stupid enough to walk into any sort of cage we might leave open for them. If you don't mind, I'll leave that as a last resort—we're going to have trouble enough getting our soil and seeds from their present containers into this thing without exposing them either to our atmosphere or to empty space. It would be a hundred times worse getting a native into one of those caves."

"Well, you may be right. I still think it would get us more tofacco, though."

"I'm sure it would, if they are at all civilized. I don't see why you're complaining about that, though—you're getting it cheap enough now, goodness knows."

"I don't mind the price—it's the quantity. We only get a couple of hundred cylinders a year—one of Three's years, that is. That doesn't let us operate on a very large scale. Well, do what you think best—provided you can convince me it's best, too." He left on that note, smiling; but the smile seemed to both Feth and Ken to have a rather unpleasant undertone. Feth looked after him a little uneasily, started to return to the job in hand, stopped once more, looked rather apologetically at Ken, and then went after Drai. The scientist remembered that Feth's last dose of the drug had come some time before his own.

That set him to wondering about when he himself could expect to feel the craving. Feth had said the interval was five or six Sarrian days—which were about thirteen Earthly hours in length. About half a day had been consumed after his first recovery in general talk, checking of the big suits, and travelling out to Three; rather more than a day in the actual tests and the meeting with which they had culminated; another half day since. Looking into the future, at least a full day must pass before the planned meeting with the natives of Three. No one could tell how long that would last, but apparently he had a couple of days' leeway in any case. He stopped worrying and turned his attention back to the partly completed vivarium.

He was not an expert welder but the specimens waiting patiently two thousand miles away would only last so long, and he did not know how long Feth would be incapacitated. He took the torch and resumed work on the outer case. He had learned from watching Feth how the testing equipment was used, and was pleasantly surprised when his seams proved airtight. That, however, was as far as he could go; the mechanic had made no written plans, and Ken had no idea of his ideas on the attachment of the various refrigerating and pumping mechanisms. He stopped work, therefore, and devoted his mind to the problem he had mentioned to Drai—how to transfer the samples to the beautiful little tank after it was completed.

He spent some time trying to invent a remote-controlled can opener before the solution struck him. Then he kicked himself soundly for not having thought of it before—his double-kneed legs gave him a noticeable advantage in that operation. After that he relaxed until Feth returned, coming as close to sleep as his race ever did.

The mechanic was back in less than four hours, as a matter of fact. He seemed to be in fairly good shape; the tofacco apparently had few visible after-effects, even after years of use, which was a comforting thing to think about.

Ken showed him what had been done on the vivarium during his absence, and Feth expressed approval. He looked a little disappointed, however, at hearing the scientist's plan for stocking the device; as it turned out, he had had one of his own.

"I don't know why we were fools enough to get the specimens before we had a place to put them," Ken said. "We run the risk of ruining them in the cans, and have the transfer problem. We'd have been a lot smarter to make this thing first, and take it down to Three's surface for stocking on the spot. Why didn't we?"

"If you want an answer to that, we were probably too eager to make the trip," was the plausible answer. "Are you going to forget about the specimens we have, then?"

"We might check their temperatures. If those are still reasonable, we might as well take them back to Three and make the transfer there. It will be interesting to see how the seeds, if any, stood their trip—not that anything will be proved if they don't come up."

"You could make a microscopic check for anything resembling seed," Feth suggested, forgetting the situation for a moment.

"Do I cook the specimen or freeze the observer?" queried the scientist in an interested tone. Feth did not pursue the matter. Instead, he turned back to his work, and gradually the vivarium took shape under his skilled tentacles. Both the refrigerator and the pump were remarkably tiny devices, each solidly attached to a side of the box-like affair. Their controls were simple; an off-on toggle for the pump, and a thermostat dial for the refrigerator.

"I haven't calibrated that," Feth said, referring to the latter. "I'm mounting a thermometer inside where it can be seen through the lid, and you'll just have to fiddle with the knob until it's right."

"That's all right—for supposedly haywire apparatus, you certainly turn out a factory job. There's nothing to apologize for that I can see."

There were several hours yet to go before they were actually due at the meeting place on Planet Three. They loafed and talked for a while, Ken's plan coming gradually into more definite shape as they did so. They discussed the peculiarities of the Planet of Ice. Feth looked through his stock cabinets and reported that there was nothing he could turn into a portable control set so that Ken could handle his own torpedo. It was his turn to kick himself when the scientist suggested that he *wire* contacts to the controls—he (Ken) did not *insist* on sending the impulses by radio. Thirty minutes later a torpedo was sitting in the shop with a long cable extending from a tiny opening in its hull, and ending in a small box with half a dozen knobs studding its surface. Ken, manipulating the knobs, found no difficulty in making the projectile do whatever he wanted.

"I guess we're even in the matter of overlooking the obvious," he said at last. "Had we better be getting ready to go?"

"I suppose so. By the way, since you can't read the torpedo's instruments, maybe you'd better let me navigate you to the ground. Then you can do what you please."

"That would be best. I certainly could not judge either distance or speed at three thousand miles from the surface."

They donned space suits, and carried their apparatus out to the *Karella*. The vivarium they left in the air lock, since it was going to have to be fastened to the torpedo anyway; but Lee found it there a little later and delivered a vitriolic comment on people who obstructed the exits from a space ship. Ken humbly carted the box inside by himself, Feth having gone up to the control room to direct the newly modified torpedo to its cradle.

They were ready to go, except for one thing, and neither of them realized the omission. It was brought home to them only a minute before the planned take-off time, when another space-suited figure glided from the air lock of the station to that of the ship. Lee waited, apparently unsurprised; and a moment later Laj Drai entered the control room.

"We may as well go, if all your apparatus is on board," he said.

Without comment, Ken nodded to the pilot.

16

Ken paused halfway into his armor to wave all four tentacles in expostulation.

"If you don't think I know what I'm talking about, why did you hire me?" he asked. "I'll get and grow plants for you as fast as I can. Our tank is only so big— there are growths down there that wouldn't fit in this ship, whether you believe it or not. I don't know any better than you what tofacco looks like when it's growing—I'm not even as sure as you seem to be that it's a plant. Just get out of your head the idea that I'm going to pack plants into this case until thay have no room to breathe, and try to develop a little patience. It took two thousand years to explore Sarr, and the exploring was a darn sight easier than this!" He resumed the task of sliding into his metal shell.

"You'll do what you're told, Mr. Ken. I don't care how you do it, as I said before; but if we're not growing tofacco in a reasonable time, someone's going to be awfully sorry."

Ken's response was slightly muffled, as only his head was now protruding from the suit. "That, of course, you can do; I can't stop you. However, if you'll let me do this my own way, I honestly think things will go faster. Use your head, after all—who does know this planet?" He paused too briefly for the question to have any but rhetorical significance, and went on: "The natives, of course. They not only know the planet, they presumably know where the tofacco can be obtained, since they sell it to you. You'll have to work hard to convince me that there's any better way of learning what we want to know than getting the information from the natives."

"But it takes so long to learn a language!"

"True. It also takes quite a while to explore two hundred million square miles of territory, even if you count out the three quarters of it that seems to be flatland—and you can't really do that; these natives may be on good enough terms with the flatlanders to get the tofacco from them by trade. How about that? I understand you had your fill of exploring the flatlands quite a while ago—what was it, nineteen out of nineteen torpedoes lost, or twenty out of twenty? The percentage was embarrassing in either case."

"But suppose they don't want us to learn where it can be obtained? They might be afraid we'd get it ourselves, instead of paying them for it."

"That would not be too stupid of them. Sure, they may suspect just that. I never denied that a certain amount of tact would be needed. If you don't think I can exercise it, I repeat—do it yourself. We have more suits. I want to go down anyway, to study the place, but come right along—the torpedo will carry you and me and the tank easily enough!"

"I may not be a genius, but I'm not completely insane. I'll be there by proxy. If I don't like your tact, you needn't bother to come back."

"Don't you want the suit? I thought they were expensive," Ken said sweetly, and pulled the massive helmet into place with a clang.

Feth, who had been listening in, dogged the piece in place. He was just a trifle worried; he himself had not talked to Drai like that for years, and still retained unpleasant memories of the last time he had done so. He knew, of course, the purpose behind Ken's attitude; the scientist wanted to annoy Drai sufficiently so that he would not suspect more than one thing at a time. That one thing was to be exactly what Ken wanted. Feth admitted to himself that that part of the conversation had been well handled. Nevertheless, he was not too sure he liked the expression of Laj Drai's face as that individual draped himself within easy earshot of the radio.

His attention was shifted from the matter as Ken called in from the air lock, reporting that he was attached.

"Let me get out of here with my own controls, and move around a bit while I'm close enough to judge results," he finished. "I'd better get the feel of this thing while I have just inertia for trouble, and before there's weight as well."

"Sound enough," Feth approved, and took his tentacles from his own controls. One eye remained on the indicators, while the other sought the nearest port. In a few seconds the cigar-shaped bit of metal came into view, darting this way and that, swinging the clumsy figure of the armored scientist from a point near its bow and the rectangular box of the vivarium a few feet farther aft—it, too, was too large to go into the cargo compartment. Ken seemed to be having no trouble in controlling the sloppy-looking assembly, and presently signified that he was ready for the dive.

"All right," Feth replied, "I have it. Be sure all your own controls are neutral—they're not cross-connected and impulses will add algebraically. By the way, *all* the stuff is in the cargo compartment."

The other torpedo with the first batch of samples had been salvaged from its lonely perch on Mercury, and Laj Drai knew that; so Feth hoped he would not notice

the slight accent on the "all." The mechanic had placed
the extra radio in with the other objects, but had done
so at the last moment and had had no time to tell Ken
about it. He hoped the fellow knew how to operate the
set.

Ken, as a matter of fact, had not realized what Feth
was implying. He was much too occupied in bracing his
nerves for the descent that had been so hard on them
the previous time. He succeeded better on this occasion,
largely because he was able to keep most of his mind on
the problems that would be facing him after he was down.
They were numerous enough.

He had little trouble finding the scene of the previous
meeting, though Feth did not succeed in lowering him
exactly over it. He was, he realized, early; the sun was
barely up. All to the good. He reported his arrival to
Feth to make sure, announced that he was resuming
control, and went to work.

His first step was to guide the torpedo downhill to
the edge of a fairly extensive patch of plant growth. Before doing anything else, he made sure that the patch
was isolated; the reaction of the vegetable matter of this
world to hot metal had impressed him strongly, and he
had a good imagination. Then he lowered the carrier
until the vivarium was touching the ground, and detached the clumsy box. The double lids opened without
difficulty—Feth had allowed for the probable effect of
low temperature on the mental hinges—and set to work.

The samples of earth came speedily from the cargo
compartment, and were dumped into the box—all at
one side. Using a strip of metal he had brought along
for the purpose, Ken levelled out the dark pile into a
layer some three inches deep and a foot wide along one
side of the container; then he began to use the strip as a
crude shovel. Tiny bushes, patches of moss, and other
growths were pried out of the ground, the scientist carefully refraining from allowing his armor to contact them
and laying the strip down to cool at frequent intervals.
He investigated the widely varying root systems, and
carefully dug an extra allowance of soil from the spot

where each plant had been removed, so that there would be a sufficient depth in the box beneath it. One by one he transferred his specimens to the vivarium, placing them much too close together to have pleased a human gardener but setting them firmly into the soil so that they stood up as they had before. Once or twice he looked longingly at larger bushes, but gave up. They were too tall, and a brief investigation showed that their roots were too long.

He had covered perhaps two of the six square feet he had to fill when the Wings arrived. Roger and Edie were noticeably in advance of the rest; the two youngest would probably have been close behind them if the scene had not been so far from home. As it was, they had begun to get a little tired, and arrived at the same time as their parents.

Ken did not hear them coming; the microphone in the torpedo was not as sensitive as it might have been, and this time Roger did not call as soon as he saw the scientist. Instead, the children came as close as they dared, trying to see what he was up to. That proved obvious enough, but it was only after his curiosity was satisfied on that point that Roger gave an audible greeting.

"I see you're here early."

"Why didn't you tell me they were coming?" snapped the voice of Laj Drai from the speaker.

"I didn't see them; I've been working," replied Ken quietly. "Now, if you expect us to get anywhere with communication, kindly keep quiet. They have no means of telling when I'm the one who's talking, and extra sounds will just confuse them." He fell silent, and watched solemnly as the rest of the human beings arrived. The size of Mr. and Mrs. Wing surprised him a little; it took him some seconds to decide that the individuals he had seen first were probably children. The adults were more impressive, if one was impressed by mere size; Ken decided that either one would outweigh the average Sarrian by fully a quarter, assuming that they really filled their queer clothing and had flesh of comparable density. There was something a little more commanding about the manner of the older natives, also; a dignity and seriousness of purpose which he now realized had been decidedly lacking in the immature specimens. For the first time, Ken really thought of the natives of Earth as possibly civilized beings.

Certainly the actions of the largest one suggested a well disciplined mind. Mr. Wing wasted little time. He seated himself in front of Ken, pulled out a notebook in which he had already noted the words Roger claimed to have taught the alien, and checked through them. He looked up at Ken as he pronounced each; the scientist responded by pointing to the appropriate object. Satisfied that these words were understood, the man promptly embarked on a language lesson with a singleness of purpose and efficiency of execution that had Ken regarding him as a fellow being long before they were in real communication. This was not accomplished at once, but it took far less time than many people would believe possible. As any proponent of Basic English will agree, most everyday matters can be discussed quite easily with a vocabulary of less than a thousand words. The present situation was not quite everyday in any sense of the term, but between Mrs. Wing's sketching ability and the willingness of the children to illustrate practically any actions required, progress was quite satisfactory to both parties.

Since Ken had stood in the same place throughout the lesson, he had warmed up the rock around his feet; consequently it was fully three hours before he felt the first warning ache of cold. When he did, however, he suddenly realized that he had done nothing toward the filling of his specimen box since the natives had arrived; and waiting courteously until Mr. Wing had finished an explanation, he indicated the dearth. The man nodded, and pointed to the ground beyond.

Ken had paid no attention to the actions of the smallest children since shortly after the lesson had started; he had judged that they were playing, as the children of his own race did. Now he was startled to see, spread out on the rock at a little distance from the case, several score plants of assorted shapes and sizes. Apparently the youngsters had seen what he was doing, and decided to help. With growing surprise, he discovered that there were no duplicates among the specimens. The race must really have brains; he had not seen either of the adults give instructions. With an oral expression of gratitude which he was sure must be lost on them, he began clumsily placing them in the box with the aid of his metal strip. As he picked up the first, he pointed to it with his free handler and said, "Word!" All understood his meaning, and Roger replied, "Fern."

After watching his clumsy actions for a moment, Mr. Wing waved him away from the box, and put the children to work. Ken watched them with tremendous interest, for the first time realizing what an efficient prehensile organ the human hand could be. The deft fingers of the girls in particular were setting the plants firmly in the earth at a rate and with an ease he himself could not have managed even without the handicap of armor and temperature difference. As each was picked up, a name was given it. It did turn out afterward that the same name had been used over several times in many cases for plants that bore either a merely superficial resemblance or none at all. It took him some time to solve that one, though he already knew that the native language had both particular and generic terms.

A very few minutes were required to cover the base of the box with neatly set plants; and not once had Ken heard the word that would have meant so much to the listening Drai. He himself was just as satisfied; the mention of "tofacco" by a native in a place where Drai could have heard it would have put a serious crimp in Ken's now rapidly maturing plans.

In spite of his having taken the cans containing the earlier specimens from the cargo section of the torpedo, it was not until he was putting the empty containers back that Ken saw the other radio Feth had placed there. For a moment he was irritated both with himself and the mechanic, since by then he had forgotten the latter's words at the time of Ken's departure; then he decided that it might be for the best. If Drai had been listening ever since the start of the language lesson, he should by now be pretty well convinced that Ken was not up to any funny business. There had been no breaks to make him suspicious.

While these thoughts were passing through his mind, Mr. Wing was also doing some thinking. It seemed fairly evident that the alien—they had not yet learned each other's names—was on the point of departure. This trip had been a pleasant enough outing for the family, it was true; but a daily repetition would be too much of a good thing, and there were more objects at their home which could be used in language instruction as well. It seemed, therefore, that it might be worth while to make the attempt he had suggested earlier to the family—persuading the aliens to land closer to the house. In consequence, when Ken turned from his task of replacing the empty cans and fastening the sealed vivarium back in place, he found the largest native facing him with a neatly drawn but quite unintelligible diagram in his hand and an evident desire to transmit intelligence of some sort.

It took four or five minutes to make clear exactly what the map represented, though Ken got the general idea after a few seconds. Scale was the principal difficulty. At last, however, the alien understood—he spent two or three minutes describing the map in detail to Feth, first, so that it could be studied and reproduced later—and then said, "Yes," to Mr. Wing.

"Tomorrow—one day after now—*here*," the man reiterated, and Ken nodded his head (he had not been too surprised to find that visual signs supplemented the spoken language of these creatures).

"Here." He indicated the same spot as well as he could with a handler, and the paper turned brown before he hastily snatched it away. Then he remembered something else. "Not tomorrow. Not one day after now. Two days." Mr. Wing frowned.

"Not tomorrow?"

"No. Two days. Go now; cold." And Sallman Ken turned, took the extra radio from the cargo compartment, placed it on the ground, said, "Carry!" and addressed himself to the task of attaching himself to the torpedo once more. He had detached himself, in spite of his original plan, when he found that he could not reach the cargo compartment while chained to the hull of the carrier.

The native mercifully said nothing as he completed this task. As a matter of fact, Mr. Wing was too dumbfounded at this turn of events to say anything; and even the children wondered how he had done it. Ken rose into the air amid a dead silence, until the two youngest children remembered their training and shrilled, "Goodbye!" after the vanishing form. He barely heard the words, but was able to guess at the meaning.

Back at the *Karella,* his first care was to get the vivarium inside. He had already evacuated the space between the walls by opening a small valve for a time during the journey through space; now he started the refrigerator, and refused to take his eyes from the inside thermometer until he had satisfied himself that all fluctuation had ceased. Then, and then only, did he start going over the tape record with Feth to make sure he remembered the hundred or so words he had been taught during his brief dive. Laj Drai, rather to Ken's surprise, forbore to interrupt, though Feth said he had listened carefully during the entire stay on the planet. During this session, Ken managed to tell the mechanic what he had done with the radio, and the latter agreed that it had been a wise move. There was now no need to fear a casual check on the contents of the torpedo by Drai or Lee.

It seemed that Ken had been more convincing than he had expected, in his speech to Drai just before leaving. He had been a little surprised when the boss had failed to interrupt him after his return; now he found that Drai had been itching to do just that, but had been afraid of putting himself in the wrong again. The moment the conference between Ken and Feth came to an end, he was at the scientist's side, asking for an eyewitness account to supplement what he had heard on the radio.

"I really need a camera to give a good idea of appearances," Ken replied. "I seem to have been wrong about their size; the ones I saw before appear to have been children. The adults are a trifle bulkier than we are.

"I don't think the language is going to be difficult, and it looks as though this group, at least, is very cooperative." He told about the help he had received in making the plant collection.

"I was looking at that," said Drai. "I don't suppose any of those things is what we're after?"

"No, unless they use different names for the living plant and the product. They named each of these to me as they set them in, and you'd have heard as well as I if they'd said 'tofacco' once." Drai seemed thoughtful for a moment before he spoke again.

"Children, eh? Maybe if you can work with them and get rid of the adults you could find things out more easily. They should be easier to fool."

"Something like that crossed my mind, too," Ken said. "Perhaps we ought to make a few more collection boxes to take down; I could give them to the kids to fill while I was having another language lesson, and then when they came back I'd have a good excuse to talk it over with each in turn. Something might very well crop up if the parents don't interfere."

"Parents? How do you know?"

"I don't, of course; but it seems likely. But what do you think of the idea?"

"Very good, I should say. Can you get enough boxes for all the children ready by their next morning?"

"I'm not going down that soon. I was making allowances for what Feth told me was the effect of tofacco on the system, and thought I might not be able to make it." Drai paused long enough to do some mental arithmetic.

"You're probably right. We'll have to go back to One to get your dose, too; I somehow can't bring myself to keep the stuff around where it might fall into the wrong hands." He smiled, with the same ugly undertone that was making Ken hate the drug-runner a little more each time he saw it.

17

"Dad, will you kindly tell me just how on Earth you worked that?" Don stared at the Sarrian radio, which was all that was visible of the aliens by the time he got back from giving the trade signal. Roger chuckled.

"He didn't work it. He spends all afternoon teaching the thing to talk English, and just as it's going it turns around and puts this on the ground. 'Carry' it booms, and takes off. What do you suppose it is, Dad?"

"I can't possibly be sure, Son, until he comes back. It may be a piece of apparatus he intends to use on his next visit; it may be a gift in return for your aid with the plant collection. I think we'd best take it home, as he seemed to want, and do nothing at all to it until he comes back."

"But if he's not coming back until the day after tomorrow—"

"I know curiosity is a painful disease, Rog; I suffer from it myself. But I still think that the one who'll come out ahead in this new sort of trading is the one who steps most cautiously and keeps his real aims up his sleeve the longest. We're still not certain that this scientific investigation isn't aimed at just one end—to relieve them of the need for paying us for tobacco. After all, why did this fellow start with plants? There are lots of other things he might have shown interest in."

"If he's as different from our sort of life as he seems to be, how would he know that tobacco is a plant?" countered Roger. "It certainly doesn't stay unburned long enough at his temperature to let him look at the crumbs with a microscope or anything, and a cigarette doesn't much look like a plant."

"That's true," his father admitted. "Well, I only said we don't *know* he hasn't that up his sleeve. I admit it doesn't seem likely."

Curiously enough, Ken thought of one of those points himself before the next visit; and when he descended in the clearing by the Wing home with four collecting boxes attached to his torpedo, the first thing he did was to make clear he wanted minerals in one that was not equipped with refrigeration apparatus. Pointing to another similarly plain he said, "Thing—good—hot—cold." The Wings looked at each other for a moment; then Edith spoke.

"You mean anything that stays good whether its hot or cold? Stuff that you don't have to keep in a refrigerator?" There were too many new words in that sentence for Ken, but he took a chance. "Yes. Hot, good." He was still drifting a foot or two from the ground, having so arranged the load this time that he could detach it without first freeing himself. Now he settled lightly to the ground, and things began to happen.

The ground, like most of that in evergreen forests, was largely composed of shed needles. These had been cleared away to some extent around the house, but the soil itself was decidedly inflammable. Naturally, the moment Ken's armored feet touched it a cloud of smoke appeared, and only lightning-like action in lifting himself again prevented its bursting into flame. As it was, no one felt really safe until Roger had soaked the spot with a bucket of water.

That led to further complications. Ken had never seen water to his knowledge, and certainly had never seen apparatus for dispensing apparently limitless

amounts of any liquid. The outside faucet from which
the bucket had been filled interested him greatly; and at
his request, made in a mixture of signs and English
words, Roger drew another bucketful, placed it on the
flat top of one of the cement posts at the foot of the
porch steps, and retreated. Ken, thus enabled to examine the object without coming in contact with anything
else, did so at great length; and finished by dipping a
handler cautiously into the peculiarly transparent fluid.
The resulting cloud of steam startled him almost as
much as the temporary but intense chill that bit through
the metal, and he drew back hastily. He began to suspect what the liquid was, and mentally took off his hat
to Feth. The mechanic, if that was all he really was,
really could think.

Eventually Ken was installed on top of an outdoor
oven near the house, the specimen boxes were on the
ground, and the children had disappeared in various directions to fill them. The language lesson was resumed,
and excellent progress made for an hour or so. At the
end of that time, both parties were slightly surprised to
find themselves exchanging intelligible sentences—
crude and clumsy ones, full of circumlocutions, but understandable. A faint smile appeared on Mr. Wing's
face as he realized this; the time had come to admin-
ister a slight jolt to his guest, and perhaps startle a little
useful information out of him. He remembered the conversation he had had with Don the night before, and felt
quiet satisfaction in the boy—the sort of satisfaction
that sometimes goes to make a father a major bore.

"You didn't have too many times, Dad," his son had
said, "but there were enough. It ties in with other
things, anyway. The intervals between signalling and the
arrival of the trading torpedo have been varying in a
period of just about a hundred and twenty days, taking
several years into account. Of course, a lot of those 'periods' didn't have any trading occur, but the period is
there; first two days, then three. That hundred and
twenty days is the synodic period of Mercury—the
length of time it takes that planet to catch the Earth up

on successive trips around the sun. I remembered Mercury's position when we studied it this spring, and did some figuring; your short times came when it was closest to us, the long ones when it was on the other side of the sun, about twice as far away. Those torpedoes seem to be coming from there at about one and a quarter G's of acceleration." Mr. Wing, though no physicist, understood this clearly enough. The concept had been publicized sufficiently in connection with airplanes.

He had looked over Don's figures, which were easy enough to follow, and agreed with his results; and the boy had, at his request, drawn a diagram of the orbits of inner planets of the Solar System showing the current positions of the planets themselves. This he now had in his pocket.

The word "home" had just been under discussion, more or less as a result of chance. Mr. Wing had made the concept reasonably clear, he believed; and it seemed to him that the time had come to put one of his cards on the table.

He began by waving an arm to encompass the whole horizon. "Earth," he said. The Sarrian repeated the word, but without any gesture of his own suggesting that he understood. The man repeated the word, stamping on the ground as he did so; then he took a new page in the notebook and made a sketch of the planet as he thought it would appear from space. As a final illustration, he molded a sphere from a lump of modeling clay which had been found in the playroom and had already been put to good use. Then he pointed to the sphere, drawing, and the ground, repeating the word after each in turn.

Ken understood. He proved it by scratching a picture of his own on the ground, reaching as far as he could over the side of the oven and using his strip of metal. It was a perfectly recognizable drawing of the sun and orbits of the first three planets. He knew he might be exceeding the local knowledge of astronomy, but the fact that the native seemed to know the shape of his world was encouraging.

Mr. Wing promptly pulled out Don's diagram, which was substantially the same as Ken's except that Mars' orbit and position were shown. He spent some minutes naming each of the planets, and making the generic name clear as well. Then they spent some more time in a sort of game; Ken added Jupiter and Saturn to the diagram, in an effort to find out how much astronomy the human being knew. Mr. Wing named those, and added Uranus, Neptune and Pluto; Don, who had made no contribution up to this point, made a correction in the orbit of Pluto so that it crossed that of Neptune at one point, and began adding satellites at a furious rate. They took the burst of Sarrian speech that erupted from the speaker as an indication of the alien's surprise, and were gratified accordingly.

Ken was surprised for more reasons than one.

"Drai, if you're listening, these folks are not any sort of savage. They must have a well-developed science. They seem to know of nine planets in this system, and we only knew about six; and there are an awful lot of moons one of them is busy telling me about right now—he's even put two with Planet Four, and we didn't notice any. They either have space travel or darned good telescopes."

"We haven't seen a space ship here in twenty years," Feth's voice reminded him. Ken made no answer; Mr. Wing had started to talk again. He was pointing to Planet Three on his own diagram, and repeating the name he had given it.

"Earth—my home." He indicated himself with one hand to emphasize the personal pronoun. Then he moved the finger to the innermost world. "Mercury—your home." And he pointed to Sallman Ken.

He was a little disappointed in the reaction, but would not have been had he known how to interpret Sarrian facial expressions. The scientist was dumbfounded for fully ten seconds; when he did regain control of his voice, he addressed the distant listeners rather than the Earthman.

"I'm sure that you will also be interested in knowing

that he is aware we come from Planet One. I believe he thinks we live there, but the error is minor under the circumstances." This time Drai's voice responded.

"You're crazy! You must have told him yourself, you fool! How could he possibly have learned that without help?"

"I did not tell him. You've been listening and ought to know. And I don't see why I should be expected to explain how he found out; I'm just telling you what's going on here at the moment."

"Well, don't let him go on thinking that! Deny it! He knows too much!"

"What's wrong with that?" Ken asked, reasonably enough.

"Suppose they do have space travel! We don't want them dropping in on us! Why—I've been keeping this place a secret for twenty years."

Ken forbore to point out the flaws in that line of reasoning. He simply said:

"Not knowing how certain they are of their facts, I think a denial would be foolish. If they are really sure, then they'd know I was lying; and the results might not be good." Drai made no answer to that, and Ken turned back to the Earthman, who had been listening uncomprehendingly to the conversation.

"Mercury. Yes," the Sarrian said.

"I see. Hot," replied Mr. Wing.

"No. Cold." Ken paused, seeking words. "Little hot. Hot to you. Hot to—" he waved a sleeve of his armor in a wide circle—"plants, these things. Cold to me."

Don muttered to his father, "If he regards Mercury as too cold for comfort, he must come from the inside of a volcano somewhere. Most astronomers are satisfied that there's no planet closer to the sun, and he didn't show one on his diagram, you'll notice."

"It would be nice if we knew just how hot he liked it," agreed the older man. He was about to address Ken again in the hope of finding out something on this point when a burst of alien speech suddenly boomed from the

torpedo's speaker. Even to Ken, it carried only partial
meaning.

"Ken! This——" Just those two words, in Feth's voice;
then the transmission ceased with the click that accom-
panies a broken circuit. Ken called Feth's name several
times into his own microphone, but there was no response. He fell silent, and thought furiously.

He suspected from the fact that the natives were simply looking at him that they realized something had
gone wrong; but he did not want to worry about their
feelings just then. He felt like a diver who had heard a
fight start among the crew of his air-pump, and had little attention for anything else. What in the Galaxy were
they about, up there? Had Drai decided to abandon
him? No, even if the drug-runner had suddenly decided
Ken was useless, he would not abandon a lot of expensive equipment just to get rid of him. For one thing,
Ken suspected that Drai would prefer to see him die of
drug hunger, though this may have been an injustice.
What then? Had Drai become subtle, and cut off the
transmitter above in the hope that Ken would betray
himself in some way? Unlikely. If nothing else, Feth
would almost certainly have warned him in some fashion, or at least not sounded so anxious in the words he
had managed to transmit.

Perhaps Drai's distrust—natural enough under the
circumstances—had reached a point where he had decided to check personally on the actions of his tame scientist. However, Ken could not imagine him trusting
himself in armor on the surface of the Planet of Ice no
matter what he wanted to find out.

Still, there was another way of coming down personally. Lee would not like it, of course. He might even
persuade his employer that it was far too dangerous. He
would certainly try. Still, if Drai really had the idea in
his mind, it was more than possible that he might simply
refuse to listen to persuasion.

In that case, the *Karella*'s shadow might fall across
them at any moment. That would fit in with Feth's attempt to warn him, and its abrupt interruption. If that

were actually the case, he need not worry; his conscience was clear, and for all that was going on at the moment Drai was perfectly welcome to look on until his
eyes froze to the ports. There had been no sign of tofacco anywhere, although the native children had been
coming back at frequent intervals with new specimens
for the boxes and had named them each time. He himself had not done a single thing in furtherance of his
plan.

He had just relaxed with this realization firmly in
mind when the native who had been doing most of the
talking produced and lighted a cigarette.

Mr. Wing had had no intention of doing anything of
the sort. He had a pretty good idea of the value placed
by these creatures on tobacco, and he did not want to
distract the scientist from what might prove a valuable
line of talk. As a matter of fact, he would have been
perfectly satisfied to have the creature assume that it
was someone else entirely who did the trading. Habit,
however, defeated his good intentions; and he was only
recalled from his speculations on the nature of this new
interruption by the realization that he had taken the
first puff.

The Sarrian had both eyes fixed on the little cylinder—an unusual event in itself; usually one was roving
in a way calculated to get on the nerves even of someone like young Roger. The reason seemed obvious; Mr.
Wing could imagine the alien running mentally over the
list of things he had brought with him, wondering what
he could trade for the rest of the pack. He was closer to
being right than he should have been.

That line of thought, however, was profitless, and no
one knew it better than Ken. The real problem of the
moment was to get the infernal stuff out of sight before
Drai arrived—if he were coming. For a moment Ken
wondered if the other radio, which he had seen lying on
the porch when he arrived, could be put to use in time.
Common sense assured him that it could not; even if he
could persuade one of the natives to bring it and tow
the torpedo out of earshot, he certainly could not make

his wish clear in time. He would have to hope—the cylinder was vanishing slowly, and there was a chance that it might be gone before the ship arrived. If only he could be sure that the receiver as well as the transmitter aboard the space ship had been cut off!

If Drai were still listening, the silence of the last few seconds would probably make him doubly suspicious. Well, there was nothing to be done about that.

As it happened, there was plenty of time for the cigarette to burn out, thanks to Ordon Lee. Feth had tried to give his warning the instant he realized what Drai was thinking; and the other's lashing tentacles had hurled him away from the board and across the control room before he could finish. When he had recovered and started to return, he had found himself staring into the muzzle of a pistol, its disc-shaped butt steadied against the drug-runner's torso.

"So the two of you *are* up to something," Drai had said. "I'm not surprised. Lee, find the carrier of that torpedo and home down on it!"

"But sir—into Three's atmosphere? We can't—"

"We can, you soft-headed field-twister. The tame brain of mine stood it for three hours and more in a suit of engineering armor, and you want me to believe the hull of this ship can't take it!"

"But the ports—and the outer drive plates—and—"

"I said *get us down there!* There are ports in a suit of armor, and the bottom plates stood everything that the soil of Planet Four could give them. And don't talk about risk from the flatlanders! I know as well as you do that the hull of this barrel is coated even against frequency-modulated radar, to say nothing of the stuff these things have been beaming out—I paid for it, and it's been getting us through the System patrol at Sarr for a long time. Now punch those keys!" Ordon Lee subsided, but he was quite evidently unhappy. He tuned in the compass with a slightly hopeful expression, which faded when he found that Ken's torpedo was still emitting its carrier wave. Gloomily he applied a driving force along the indicated line, and the gibbous patch of light that was Planet Three began to swell beyond the ports.

As the board flashed a warning of outside pressure, he brought the vessel to a halt and looked hopefully at his employer. Drai made a downward gesture with the gun muzzle. Lee shrugged in resigned fashion, switched on the heaters in the outer hull, and began feeling his way into the ocean of frigid gas, muttering in an under-tone and putting on an I-told-you-so expression every time a *clink* told of contracting outer plates.

Feth, knowing he would get no further chance at the radio, glued his attention to one of the ports. One of Drai's eyes did likewise, but no change appeared in his expression as the evidence began to pile up that Ken had been telling the truth. Great mountains, hazy air, green vegetation, even the shiny patches so suggestive of the vast blue plains where the flatlanders had downed the exploring torpedoes; all were there, as the scientist had said, dimly illuminated by the feeble sun of this sys-tem but clearly visible for all that. Feth, heedless of the gun in Drai's hand, suddenly leaped for the door, shout-ing, "Camera!" and disappeared down the corridor. Drai put the gun away.

"Why can't you be like those two?" he asked the pi-lot. "Just get them interested in something, and they forget that there's anything in the universe to be afraid of." The pilot made no immediate answer; apparently Drai expected none, for he strolled to the port without waiting. Then without looking up from his controls the pilot asked sourly:

"If you think Ken is interested in his job and nothing else why are you so anxious to check up on him all of a sudden?"

"Mostly because I'm not quite sure whose job he's doing. Tell me, Lee, just who would you say was to blame for the fact that this is the first time we're land-ing on this world which we've known about for twenty years?"

The pilot made no verbal answer, but one eye rolled back and met one of his employer's for a moment. The question had evidently made him think of something other than frostbite and cracked plates: Laj Drai may not have been a genius, as he had been known to admit, but his rule-of-thumb psychology was of a high order.

The *Karella* sank lower. Mountain tops were level with the port now; an apparently unbroken expanse of green lay below, but the compass pointed unhesitatingly into its midst. At five hundred feet separate trees were discernible, and the roof of the Wing home showed dimly through them. There was no sign of Ken or his torpedo, but neither being in the control room doubted for an instant that this was the house he had mentioned. Both had completely forgotten Feth.

"Take us a few yards to one side, Lee. I want to be able to see from the side ports. I think I see Ken's armor—yes. The ground slopes; land us uphill a little way. We can see for a fair distance between these plants." The pilot obeyed silently. If he heard the shriek of Feth, echoing down the corridor from the room where the mechanic was still taking pictures, he gave no sign; the words were rendered indistinguishable by reverberation in any case. The meaning, however, became clear a moment later. The sound of the hull's crushing its way through the treetops was inaudible inside; but the other token of arrival was quite perceptible. An abrupt cloud of smoke blotted out the view from port, and as Laj Drai started back in astonishment a tongue of flame licked upward around the curve of the great hull.

18

Feth was not the only one who called to the pilot to hold off. Ken, realizing only too clearly that the hull of the vessel would be nearly as hot as his own suit in spite of its superior insulation, expressed himself on the radio as he would never have done before his pupils; but of course no one on board was listening. Mr. Wing and Don, guessing the cause of his excitement, added their voices; Mrs. Wing, hearing the racket, appeared at a window in time to see the glossy black cylinder settle into the trees fifty yards above the house. No one was surprised at the results—no one outside the ship, at least.

Don and his father raced at top speed for the stable, where the portable fire pumps were kept. Mrs. Wing appeared on the porch, calling in a fairly well controlled voice, "Don, where are the children?" This question was partially answered before either man could make a response, as Margie and Billy broke from the woods on opposite sides of the clearing, still carrying plants which they had forgotten to drop in their excitement.

"Daddy! See the fire!" the boy shrilled as soon as he saw his father.

"I know, Billy. Both of you go with your mother, start the pump, and help her spray everything near the house. I don't think the fire will come downhill with the wind the way it is, but we mustn't take chances."

"Where are Roger and Edith?" Mrs. Wing asked the younger children.

"They were going to get rocks for the fire-man," Margie replied. "I don't know where they were going to get them. They'll come back when they see the fire."

"I suppose so." Their mother was obviously unhappy about the matter, but she took the youngsters in tow and went after the hoses. Don and his father continued on their way, slung the always filled fire pumps across their shoulders, and headed back uphill toward the ever-thickening cloud of smoke and flame.

Ken had not waited for the human beings to go into action. Pausing only to make certain his armor was still firmly attached to the torpedo, he had seized the control spindle and shot straight upward. He was taking a chance, he realized; but with the relatively cold torpedo hull to smash the initial path through the thin overhanging branches he felt that he could avoid contact with any one of them except for periods too brief to set them ablaze. He succeeded, though a suspicion of smoke floated upward in his wake as he soared clear. The *Karella,* he noted, had done likewise; it now floated a quarter of a mile above the blaze it had started. He wasted no further time on recriminations, even though the chances seemed good that those on board would be listening again.

The fire was not spreading as rapidly as he had feared it might in most directions. On the side toward the house it seemed to have made no progress at all, while along the contours of the mountain its advance was very slow. Upward, however, under the combined influence of its own convection currents and the breeze which had already been blowing in that direction, it was leaping from growth to growth in fine style. Ken saw flaming bits of vegetable tissue borne far aloft on the hot air pillar; some burned out in flight, others settled into the trees farther up the mountain and gave rise to other centers of combustion. A dark-colored growth, apparently dead, a few yards in advance of the main blaze, smoked briefly in the fierce radiation and suddenly exploded with an audible roar, burning out in less than fifteen seconds and crumbling into a rain of glowing coals. Ken, unmoved by the prospect of being in-volved in the uprushing hot gases, maneuvered closer to the blaze. At least part of the reason for the slow ad-vance downhill became evident; the two natives with whom he had been talking were visible through the trees, spraying everything in sight with apparently tiny streams of a liquid at whose nature Ken could only make an educated guess. He watched them for some time, noting that they refilled their containers of liquid every few minutes at a stream of the stuff flowing down near the house, which Ken had not noticed earlier. He wondered where the liquid could have its source, and decided to follow the stream uphill to find out.

As he rose, the extent of the forest country once more was impressed on him, and he began to wonder at the magnitude of the catastrophe the *Karella* had caused. If this combustion reaction were to spread over the whole countryside, the effect on the natives would undoubtedly be quite serious, he decided. He noted that it had spread across the little stream a short distance farther up; apparently the liquid had to be in actual contact with vegetation in order to stop combustion. The flame and smoke made it impossible to follow the watercourse; Ken dropped lower, reasoning with some justice that the temperature of his armor would do no damage to vegetation already burning, and drifted along only a few feet above the stream bed, barely able to see even then. For the first time he saw animal life other than the intelligent natives; tiny creatures, usually four-legged when they were moving slowly enough for him to see the legs, all fleeing madly uphill. Ken wondered that they could breath—the smoke suggested that the air should be full of combustion products, and probably was too hot for them; he knew nothing about the fairly common phenomenon of relatively pure air near the ground ahead of a fire. Large scale conflagrations oc-curred on Sarr, but he was no fireman.

He was ahead of the flames but still in smoke-filled air when he found the source of the stream. He had trouble realizing that it *was* the source; he was no geolo-

gist, and a real geologist of his race would have had
difficulty in figuring out the mechanism of a spring.
Ken rather suspected artificial backing for the phenomenon, but he did not dare touch the liquid to investigate
very closely. He would have had grounds for serious
worry had he known that a forest fire can sometimes
cause a local rainstorm; but that, too, was too far outside his experience. The closest approach to such a
thing on Sarr occurred near the poles, where on very
rare occasions meteorological forces so combined as to
raise the pressure and drop the temperature enough to
cause a slight precipitation of liquid sulfur.

Realizing that nothing more could be learned here at
the moment, Ken rose once more into clearer air.
Downhill, the natives seemed to be winning; there was a
narrow band of blackened vegetation at the edge of the
region of flame which suggested that the fire had
burned out in that direction. At the sides, progress was
less obvious; but the fire in general had taken on the
outline of a great fan, with its handle pointing toward
the house and the ribs spreading to a breadth of three
or four hundred yards at a roughly equal distance up
the mountainside. Through the billowing smoke, Ken
could see that the large trees were thinning out at this
point, giving way to smaller growths which in turn
seemed to follow the usual pattern of yielding to bare
rock near the top of the hill. Ken, looking the situation
over from his vantage point, decided that the blaze
stood a very good chance of eating itself into starvation
territory in a very few hours; the natives might very well
dispose of the fringes without assistance.

The thought of possible assistance gave rise to another; the smoke was rising in a pillar that must be visible for many miles. Was this likely to bring other natives to help, or would it be mistaken for an ordinary
cloud? Ken's eyes, with their color balance differing as
it did from the human, could not be sure of the distinc-
tion in hue; but the shape of the smoke pillar seemed
distinctive enough to attract attention. With this thought
in mind, he decided to call the ship; but when he looked

up, the vessel was nowhere in sight. He moved the torpedo back and forth rapidly enough to cause his armor to swing pendulum fashion and give him a glimpse of the sky directly overhead, but there was still no sign of the black cylinder. Apparently Laj Drai's brief taste of Planet Three had been enough. To make sure, Ken broadcast his thought on the matter of further natives arriving, and then returned to his examination of the fire. Within seconds, he had once more forgotten the vessel's existence.

He had found that little could be seen inside the fire itself. This time, therefore, he descended just ahead of the actual blaze, watching through the eddying smoke clouds as the leaves of bushes and small trees in its path shriveled, smoked, and burst into flame sometimes many feet from the nearest actual tongue of fire. Usually, he noticed, the thicker stems did not ignite until they were actually in contact with flame from some other source, but there were exceptions to this. He remembered the exploding tree. He regretted that he had no thermometer, with which he could get some idea of the kindling point of the growths. He wondered if the oxygen alone could be responsible for such a furious reaction, or whether the nitrogen which made up such a large part of the atmosphere might be playing a part. It had combined with his titanium specimen, after all. There seemed no way of collecting samples of the combustion gases, but perhaps some of the solid residue would tell. Ken landed in the midst of the fire, brought the torpedo down beside him, opened the cargo door, and threw in several pieces of charred wood. Then he went downhill a short distance, located some grayish ash, and added that to the collection. Satisfied for the moment, he rose clear of the ground again, wondering vaguely how much time, if any, his brief sojourn in the flames would add to the few hours he could remain down. He had heard the thermostats in his armor cutting off several of the heaters during those few minutes; the outer layers must have been warmed up considerably.

In an attempt to guess how long the fire would take to burn out, Ken moved fifty or sixty yards ahead of the flame front and began timing its rate of progress at several points. This proved deceptive, since the rate of travel varied greatly—as any forester could have told him. It depended principally on the sort of fuel available in a given spot and on the configuration of the ground, which influenced the air currents feeding the fire; and those points were both too difficult to observe for Ken to learn very much about them. He gave up that attempt, moved a little farther ahead, and tried to see what he could of the animals still scurrying away from the most frightful menace that ever threatened their small lives.

It was here that the torpedo microphone picked up a cracking that differed from that of the fire, and a heavy panting that reminded Ken of the sounds he had heard just after his first meeting with Roger. Remembering that he had not seen two of the natives just after the blaze had started, the scientist became a trifle anxious; and two or three minutes' search showed that his worry was only too well founded. Roger and Edith Wing, gasping and coughing from smoke and exhaustion, were struggling almost blindly through the bushes. The boy's original intention had been to travel across the path of the blaze, to get out of its way—the most sensible course under the circumstances. Several things, however, had combined to make this a trifle difficult. For one thing, after the smoke had become thick enough to prevent their seeing more than a few yards, they had blundered into a little hollow. Using the slope of the ground for guidance, they had made several complete circles of this spot before realizing what had happened. By that time the flames were actually in sight, and they had no choice but to run straight before them. They simply did not know by then how wide the flame front was; to parallel it at a distance of only a few yards would have been the height of insanity. They had been trying to work their way to one side while keeping ahead of the flames, but they were rapidly approaching a state of exhaustion where merely keeping ahead demanded all that their young bodies could give. They were nearly blind, with tears streaming down their soot-stained faces. In Edith's case the tears were not entirely due to smoke; she was crying openly from fatigue and terror, while the boy was having a good deal of trouble keeping his self-control.

None of these facts were very clear to the scientist, since even the undistorted human face was still quite strange to him; but his sympathy was aroused just the same. It is possible that, had the same situation occurred just after his first meeting with the natives, he might have remained an impassive observer in order to find out just what the creatures would and could do in an extremity. Now, however, his talk with Mr. Wing and the evidence of culture and scientific knowledge the native had shown gave the Sarrian a feeling of actual intellectual kinship with the creatures below him; they were people, not animals. Also, they had fallen into their present plight while working for him; he remembered that these two had departed in search of specimens for him. He did not hesitate an instant after seeing them.

He dropped toward the stumbling children, using one of his few English verbs for all it was worth. "Carry!" the torpedo speaker boomed, again and again. He stopped just ahead of the startled youngsters, poised just out of contact with the vegetation. Edith started to reach toward him, but Roger still retained some presence of mind.

"No, Edie! You'll be burned that way, too. We'll have to ride the thing that carries him, if we can get up to it." Ken had already realized this, and was manipulating his control spindle in an effort to bring the torpedo's tail section within their reach, while he himself was still supported safely above the bushes. He had no intrinsic objection to igniting them, since they were doomed in a few minutes anyway, but it looked as though the young natives were going to have trouble enough without an extra fire right beside them. The problem was a little awkward, as his armored feet hung two yards below the hull of the torpedo, and the carrier itself contained automatic circuits designed to keep it horizontal while hovering in a gravitational field. It could be rotated on any axis, however; the main trouble was that Ken had had no occasion to do so as yet, and it took a little time to solve the necessary control combination. It seemed like an hour, even to him, before he succeeded in the maneuver, for he had thrown his full heart into the rescue and was almost as anxious as the children themselves; but at last the rear end of the yard-thick cylinder hung within its own diameter of the ground.

The children at once made frantic efforts to climb aboard. They had no luck; the composition was too slippery, the curve not sharp enough to afford a real grip, and they themselves too exhausted. Roger made a hand-stirrup for his sister, and actually succeeded in getting her partly across the smooth hull; but after a moment of frantic, futile clutching she slipped back and collapsed on the ground, sobbing. Roger paused, indecisive. A blast of hot, smoky air made him gasp for breath; there remained bare moments, it seemed to him, before the flames would be on them. For a second he stared enviously at the helpless being hanging from the other end of the torpedo, to whom the fire's breath was probably a cooling breeze; then he saw the clamps from which the specimen boxes had hung.

For a moment even these seemed useless. He doubted whether he could hang by hand grip alone from those small metal projections for any length of time, and was sure his sister in her present condition could not do so for a moment. Then he had an idea. The clamps were really hook-like, lockable devices rather like the clasp of a brooch; fastened, they made complete rings. Roger fastened the nearest, pulled his belt off with a savage jerk, threaded it through the ring, and buckled it again. Hastily urging Edie to her feet—she gained a little self-possession as she saw what he was doing—he did the same with her belt in another

ring, not stopping to give thanks that she was wearing
dungarees. All the children did in the woods. Then he
helped support her while she held to one of the loops of
leather and thrust both legs through the other. Some
work would still be needed to hold on, but the leg-strap
was carrying most of her weight. Satisfied, he waved the
Sarrian off.

Ken understood, and his admiration for the human
race went up another notch or two. He did not hesitate
or argue, however; he knew perfectly well that the boy
had found the only likely method of transporting either
of them, and even if Ken could speak his language well
enough argument would be a waste of time. He took off
at once, the dazed girl hanging behind him.

He rose first out of the smoke, to give his passenger a
chance to breath; then he took a good look at his surroundings, to be sure of finding the spot again. A mo-
mentary break in the smoke below showed Roger struggling uphill once more; and without waiting for further
observation Ken sent the torpedo plunging downhill toward the house. Mrs. Wing saw them coming, and he
was on his way back for a second load in three quarters
of a minute.

In spite of the brief interval and his careful observa-
tions, he realized as he arrived overhead that finding
the other native was not to be an easy job. His original
point of observation was reached easily enough; but he
discovered when he arrived there that with the total
lack of instruments at his disposal and the moderately
strong and erratic air current obviously present there
was no way for him to tell whether he had risen vertically to that point, or whether he would be descending
vertically from it. He had, of course, seen Roger after
getting there, but the boy had already been in motion.
He could also cut his lift entirely and fall vertically; but
that line of action did not recommend itself. The torpedo was a heavy machine, and he had no desire to
have it drop on his armor, especially in the gravity of
this planet. He did the best he could, letting down to

ground level as rapidly as seemed safe and starting a regular search pattern over the area.

Where he landed, the fire had not quite reached, though the bushes were beginning to smoke. There was no trail such as the boy might have left, or at least none that Ken could recognize. Playing safe, he moved downhill to the very edge of the fire and searched back and forth across it for fifty yards each way—a considerable distance, when the visibility was less than a tenth of that. Then he began moving his sweep gradually up the hill.

Roger had made more progress than might have seemed likely, considering the condition in which Ken had left him; it was fully ten minutes before the scientist found him, still struggling on but making practically no headway. He must have actually gained on the fire during at least part of that time, however, the Sarrian realized.

He sent his booming call downward, and once more lowered the tail of the torpedo. Roger, with a final effort, got his legs through one of the straps, and folded his arms through the other. His face was within an inch or two of the torpedo hull, which had been heated considerably by its recent passage along the flame front; but anything was better than staying where he was, and Roger was scarcely conscious of the blistering on his hands and face. Ken, once sure that the boy had a good grip, plunged up into clear air and bore his second burden down to the house. Roger was still holding on when they arrived, but it was hardly a conscious effort—his mother had to unlock his frantic grip by force.

Ken, knowing he could do no good around the house, went back uphill above the treetops to see how the others were making out in their fire fighting, leaving the presumably competent adult to care for the rescued children. The need for effort seemed to be decreasing; the lower portion was definitely burned out, it seemed to him, and the only activity was along the upper edge. The men were still at work soaking down the edges as they worked upward, but the really lively area had long since outrun them. It was, as Ken had rather expected, heading for bare rock and fuel starvation; but it would be many hours yet before it died completely. As the Wings were perfectly aware, it would be a source of danger for days if the wind should shift, and they did not let up for an instant in their effort until forced to do so by sheer exhaustion. Twice during that period Ken landed on bare patches near Mr. Wing and sketched a rough map of the situation on the ground. Once he hugged ground between trees himself for many minutes while a stiff-winged, three-engined metal machine droned overhead; again he concealed himself as a group of men, bearing water pumps and other fire-fighting tools appeared on the trail from Clark Fork and passed on uphill to help. Ken remained in the vicinity of the house after that; he did not particularly want to be seen by these new natives, reasoning that much delay to his language progress would ensue. He may have been right.

It was shortly after the arrival of the new group that Mr. Wing and Don appeared at the house, almost ready to drop. They were scratched, soot-stained, and scorched; even Ken could appreciate the difference from their former appearance, for they appeared in even worse shape than Roger and Edie had been. It was then, for the first time, that Mr. Wing learned of the danger and rescue of the two, for Ken had made no attempt to apprise him of the matter—it was too difficult, with his limited grasp of English, to manufacture adequate phrases.

Mr. Wing had the same trouble, after he heard the story. Ken had already judged that the race must have strongly developed ties of affection; now he was sure of it. Mr. Wing could not find the words to express himself, but he made the fact of his gratitude amply clear.

19

The *Karella* had indeed left the earth's atmosphere, but had not returned to her previous height. Two-way communication had been reestablished—Ken wished he knew just when—and Feth was once more controlling the torpedo which carried the scientist. The process of getting aboard was no more complicated than usual. Ken left the two "live" boxes in the air lock for the time being, having set their refrigerators to the same power as the first had seemed to require; the other two, partly filled with mineral specimens, he brought inside. Drai greeted him rather sourly as he emerged from his metal chrysalis.

"So you're finally back. What did you get, if anything?" Ken eyed him with the closest approach to a defiant expression he had yet worn.

"Very little. Thanks to the slight distraction you seem to have engineered, the natives had other things to do than talk to me."

"How was I to know that the ship's hull would set off a chain reaction in the local vegetation? I should think if anything could to it, it would have happened long ago from some other cause."

"I seem to recall telling you of the danger myself. And it may have happened before; the natives seemed to have fairly well organized means of dealing with it."

"Then the fire is out?"

"Not quite. It will probably react for some hours yet. What I dislike is your habit of assuming that I am either a liar or a fool. I told you what happened to the piece of vegetation I picked up; I told you what I was doing with the native in the matter of learning his language. You were listening to me most if not all of the time. What possessed you to come down the way you did?"

"Because I doubted what you told me." Drai made the statement without circumlocution; he apparently felt he was on secure ground. "You said that there had been no talk between you and the native on the subject of tofacco; you even said that you doubted that this was the same native we've been trading with."

"I said I wasn't sure he *was* the same. That's minor, though—go ahead."

"The first day, while you were down talking to him, the signal came from the fixed transmitter, indicating that they were ready to trade."

"I should think that would support my veracity. I was not near the transmitter. Ask Feth—he landed me."

"That's what I thought, for a while. But today, which was the usual interval after a signal, I sent down another torpedo while you were having your 'language lesson'—and nothing happened! There was no one there."

"You mean no one gave you any tofacco."

"No one took the metal, either. I'd be willing to believe they were trying to cheat me, if it had gone without anything in return; but that doesn't fit. I decided you had let something slip while I wasn't listening, and came down to see what you were up to."

"Skipping for the moment the question of how I could possibly tell whether or not you were listening, I'm not sure whether to be glad you think me stupid rather than dishonest. I agree that my native may be your trader, in that case; he might have decided to go to the transmitter later in the day, after he had talked to me. He knew I couldn't stay long. In that case, you have only yourself to thank that he didn't go later—he was too busy. Also, a couple of the young ones were nearly killed by the chain reaction; he may not be too pleased with you now, if he's connected the ship and the

trading business. After all, remember he knows we
come from Planet One on these trips."

"That I don't believe. He couldn't possibly know it.
That's another reason I decided you were trying to
cover up your own indiscretion. How do you know that
two of the natives were endangered by the fire?"

"I saw them. As a matter of fact, I rescued them—
rode them out of the way on the torpedo. I spent quite a
while investigating the whole thing, since once you'd
started it there there was nothing else for me to do. I
can prove that—I got some specimens of vegetation residue that may give some more information about the
planet." Drai eyed him silently for some moments.

"I'm not convinced yet, and you'd better convince me
before your next drug-hunger comes due. If they're
going to stop trading, I'm going to stop distributing free
samples." Feth, in the background, emitted an uncon-
trolled sound that was the equivalent of a gasp of dis-
may; Ken permitted an anxious expression to reach his
face for a moment. He had had one brief experience of
tofacco-hunger now, and did not want a prolonged one.
Drai nodded as he saw the expression. "Yes. The stock
is not very high, and if it's to be the last, I'm going to
get value for it. I have been given an idea from what
you just told me. If this tale of having rescued two natives from death by overheating is true, you can just go
back down and play on their gratitude. You can make
out that *you* want to trade for tofacco. Surely they will
gratify the hero who pulled them from terrible death.
Particularly if he makes it clear that he's in for a very
uncomfortable time if they don't. You go right back
down—your armor's warmed up by this time. We haven't
pulled in the other torpedo yet; as soon as you go
on local control down there, we'll send it over to you
with the metal, and you can haggle to your heart's con-
tent." He ceased, still wearing a definite sneer.

"That fact that my knowledge of the language is still
fragmentary does not bother you?"

"No. I think you know more than you say."

"How about the fact that there are, at the moment,

many other natives at the scene of the fire? I kept among the trees when they arrived so as not to be seen, but I can't do that and trade at the same time. Do you want me to work out in the open? They'll all be fire-fighting for a while, but I suppose they'll want metal afterward." He paused. "I don't see how they can *all* be the one you've been trading with. But I suppose you don't mind opening new bargains with the others—" Laj Drai interrupted.

"You can wait."

"Oh, it wouldn't take very many torpedo loads of metal to satisfy them all, I'm sure."

"I said you could wait." Drai must have seen the satisfied expression that flickered for an instant on the scientist's face, for he added, "I have another idea. The *Karella* will go down with you, and both watch and listen. Possibly if the native becomes recalcitrant, we can suggest lighting another fire."

"Now you want the natives to get a good look at a full-sized space ship. You don't care much about the law, do you?"

"You ought to know. Besides, they've seen it already. However, we'll wait—for a while. I rather think we'll land at a little distance from the scene of the fire, and drop in when it's out. That way," both eyes fixed themselves on Ken, "we'll be sure who talks, and for how long." He turned, pushed off from a convenient wall, and glided out of sight along the corridor. Feth followed him with one troubled eye.

"Ken, you shouldn't use that tone of voice to him. I know you don't like him—no one could—but remember what he can do. I thought, after you'd had a taste of that, you'd calm down a bit. Now he's likely to hold out on you just for the fun of it."

"I know—I'm sorry if I've gotten you in trouble too," replied the scientist. "I just think he's safer when angry. While he's gone, now, we'll have to talk fast. There's work to be done. First of all, was he telling the truth about the short supply of tofacco? Does he keep it all in that refrigerated safe that he hands out our doses from?"

"Yes. And he's probably telling the truth; most of the stuff goes back to the Sarrian system at the end of the season, and he doesn't keep much on hand."

"How much constitutes a dose? I didn't get a really good look at what was inside the brick of frozen air, either time."

"A little cylinder about so big." Feth illustrated. "It comes that way, only in longer sticks—he cuts them into ten sections, and freezes each one up for a separate dose."

"All right—that's what I wanted to make sure of. Now, how good are the little refrigerators on those vivaria of mine? Will they freeze air?"

"Sure. Why?"

"You'll see. Right now, I imagine I have another acting job to do; I don't suppose anything would stop Drai from going down to the surface of Three, as he said." Without explaining anything more, Ken headed toward the control room of the interstellar flyer.

He was quite right; the impatient drug-runner had already ordered the pilot down once more. Lee was making no objection this time, though his expression was not actually one of delight. The descent was uneventful, practically a repetition of the earlier one, except that they were homing on the fixed transmitter and consequently were some eight miles east of their former point of landing. They stopped at a height of two miles above the nearest peaks, and looked around for the smoke cloud. Rather to Drai's disappointment, they saw it; even their eyes could distinguish it from the regular clouds without much difficulty.

"It still seems to be burning," Ken remarked innocently. "Are we going to drift here in full sight until they put it out?"

"No. We'll go down and hide."

"Among the plants? That doesn't seem to work so well, as a method of concealing this ship." Drai eyed the scientist for some time, obviously near the limit of exasperation.

"I'm looking after the matter, thank you. The vegetation does not grow everywhere, as even you should be able to see. There, for example." He pointed to the south. A triangular patch which gave a metallic reflection of the sky light lay in that direction. It was one of those Ken had noticed on his first descent. "We'll look that over. It seems to be lower than the surrounding territory, and would make a very good hiding place. If it's really like the sort of ground the flatlanders live on, these other natives may very well avoid it. How about that, scientist?"

"You seem to have some logic on your side," Ken replied equably. Drai made no answer to this; he simply gestured to Lee, and the pilot obediently slanted their line of descent toward the shiny patch.

With radio altimeter registering five hundred feet, Ken began a careful examination of the area. It was larger than he had guessed from a distance, and he found himself unable to decide on its nature. The planet had some queer minerals, of course; the brief look he had had of the specimens he had just brought in showed that. Directly below he could make out no details at all; but over near the edge of the area, the trees that rimmed it were reflected—

"Lee! Hold up!" The pilot obeyed without thought, stung by the urgency of his tone.

"What is it?" The eternal suspicion was lacking even from Drai's voice, this time.

"It's a liquid—see how the reflection at the edge trembles in the air currents!"

"So what?"

"The only liquid I've encountered on this planet behaved an awful lot like that queer oxide we found on Four—the one that nearly froze my feet. I saw some before here, and dipped a handler in it; the stuff vaporized instantly, and it was minutes before I could put a tentacle in the sleeve again. I think it's that heat-drinking stuff—hydrogen oxide."

"Why didn't you mention this before?" The suspicion was back in Drai's tone.

"What chance have I had? Besides, I don't care if you leave yourself a frozen memorial on this planet—it's just that I'm with you at the moment. If you don't want to believe me, at least put a torpedo down on it first. You must have plenty of those."

Even Drai could find no fault with this suggestion, and he gestured to Feth. The mechanic, with a censorious glance at Ken, went to his control board and without comment launched another of the projectiles. The one Ken had used was available, but it was the only one fitted with manual control, and he did not want to waste it. He was already convinced of the correctness of Ken's hypothesis.

The slim projectile appeared outside the control room port, and drifted gently down to the surface of the lake. It was still hot, having been stowed inside the ship; and contact with the liquid surface was heralded by a burst of steam. Feth hastily lifted it a short distance, and waited for it to cool somewhat.

"Hardly a fair test to cool it off that fast," he said. "Something's bound to give."

Presently he lowered the machine again. This time only ripples marked the contact. Very cautiously Feth forced it still lower, while the others watched silently. Apparently the cold did not matter.

But something else did. Quite suddenly another cloud of steam arose, and a wave of considerable size spread from the place where the torpedo had been. *Had been* was the right expression; there was no response when the mechanic manipulated the controls to bring it up again. He glanced up, presently.

"It's a pity that only the cargo compartments of those things are airtight. Apparently the liquid bothers electrical machinery. Maybe it dissolves insulation." Laj Drai was looking as though he had seen a ghost. He made no direct answer to the mechanic's remark.

"Ken!" he spoke suddenly, still looking preoccupied.

"When you first described this patch of stuff, you said its appearance reminded you of the flat country. Right?"

"Right." Ken saw what the drug-runner had in mind.

"Would it—would it be possible for a planet to have so much liquid that three quarters of its surface would be covered?"

"I certainly can't say it's impossible. I admit it's hard to imagine. Any liquid at all—and particularly something as rare as that stuff is with us. Still, this is a larger planet than Sarr, and would have a greater velocity of escape, and is colder, so the average speed of the gas molecules would be slower—let's see—" His voice trailed off as he became involved in mental arithmetic. "Yes, this planet would hold the stuff easily enough; and hydrogen and oxygen are common elements in the universe. I'm afraid it's very possible, Drai." The other did not answer; everyone else knew what he was thinking. When he did speak, Ken felt smug—he had predicted the subject correctly.

"But the flatlanders—could they live in the stuff?— but maybe there aren't any; the liquid must have destroyed the torpedoes—but their radar beams! We've detected those!" He looked at Ken suddenly, as though he had made a telling point in an argument. Ken had been following his thoughts well enough to answer.

"You have no evidence whatever that those beams were not generated by the same race with which you have been trading. I have already pointed out that they are competent astronomers. I think you have been developing a very interesting mythology for the last twenty years, though I admit the idea could do with a little more proof."

Keeping one eye on the enigmatic liquid beyond the port, Drai rolled the other toward the pilot.

"Lee, go up about ten miles, and start travelling. It doesn't matter which way, I guess." He was obeyed in silence. Even though Lee did not take the shortest route to the ocean, the speed of the ship even within the

atmosphere was such that only minutes passed before
the fabulous "flatland" lay beneath them—the closest
any of them had dared to approach it in twenty Sarrian
years. Dumbly the commander gestured downward, and
presently they hung a few hundred feet above the
waves. Drai looked for a long time, then spoke three
words to Ken: "Get a sample."

The scientist thought for a moment; then he found
the small bomb in which he had taken the frost sample
on Mars, pumped out the air, and closed the valve. Re-
donning his armor, he clumped into the air lock after
voicing dire warning to Lee about keeping the vessel
level. He fastened a wire to the bomb itself and another
to the valve handle; then, opening the outer door, he
lowered away until the loss of weight told him the bomb
was submerged. He pulled the other wire, waited a moment, pulled up the filled bomb, closed the valve again,
and sealed the outer door of the air lock.

Naturally, the bomb exploded violently within a few
seconds of the time that sulfur ceased condensing on its
surface. Ken felt thankful that he had not yet removed
the armor—parts of the bomb had actually scored the
metal—and after some thought tried again. This time he
let down a tiny glass wool sponge, hoping the liquid had
a significant amount of natural capillary action. He
placed the sponge in another bomb, and by the same
method he had used with the Martian sample eventually
determined the molecular weight of the substance. It
came out higher than before, but eventually he found
the deposit of salts on the sponge and allowed for their
weight. The result this time left little doubt that the
substance was indeed hydrogen oxide.

He looked down for a minute at the tossing blue expanse, wondering how deep it might be and whether it
would have any real effect on the conditions of the
Planet of Ice; then he turned, climbed out of the armor—he had stayed in it for the rest of his experiment,
after the first blast—and went to report to Drai.

The drug-runner heard him in silence. He still
seemed a little dazed by the overthrow of his former

belief. It was many minutes before he spoke, and then he simply said, "Take us back to One, Lee. I have to think." Ken and Feth eyed each other, but kept all expression of glee from their faces.

20

"Well, you seem to have done it now." Feth was still unhappy.

"In what way?" queried Ken. The two were ostensibly engaged in checking the mechanical adequacy of the refrigerated vivaria.

"I've been working for years to support this flatland myth—I realized it was never more than a theory, but Drai had to be shown the difference between that and fact—and I've been doing my level best to keep the production of tofacco down to a minimum."

"Provided it was not cut off entirely," Ken interjected rather unkindly.

"True. Now you blow up the story that kept him scared of really exploring the planet, and at the same time give him a tool for getting what he wants from the inhabitants by threats and force. If you had any ideas in mind at all, they seem to have flopped badly."

"Oh, I wouldn't say that. You saw the way Drai was feeling when he left the ship."

"Oh, yes, he was regretting the wasted years and the money that went with them, I suppose. That won't last much longer; he's been mooning for days now. Then he'll—" Ken had been thinking furiously as the me-

chanic delivered his gloomy discourse; now he interrupted abruptly.

"Then he'll be too late to do anything. Feth, I want
you to take me on trust for a while. I promise you won't
miss your sniff. I'm going to be very busy in the air lock
for at least a couple of hours, I imagine. Lee is still
aboard. I want you to find him, and keep him occupied
in any way you see fit for at least that length of time. I
don't want him to see what I'm doing. You have known
him longer than I, and can figure out something to interest him. Just don't kill him; we're going to need him
later."

Feth looked at the scientist for several seconds, obviously doubtful. Ken wisely said nothing more, letting
him fight his own battle with a perfectly natural fear.
He was pleased but not too surprised when the mechanic finally said, "All right," and disappeared toward
the control room. Ken waited a moment; then, reasonably sure of not being interrupted, he closed the inner
door of the air lock, donned a regular space suit, and
set briskly to work. He was rather regretful of the need
for sacrificing some of his living specimens, but he con-
soled himself with the thought they could easily be replaced later. Then, too, the vivarium he had to use was
the one containing only a few plants—the fire had interrupted before the human children had made much
progress with it. That was foresight, not good fortune;
he had had to decide which of them he was going to
use, before he had left the planet.

In the control room, Feth did not find his task too
difficult. He was not on the best of terms with the pilot,
but had never held toward him the blazing hatred he
had felt toward his chief. Lee was not particularly scru-
pulous, as he had shown in the past, but Feth knew of
nothing in his record to call forth whole-souled detesta-
tion. In consequence, there was nothing strange in the
mechanic's entering the control room and settling down
for a talk. The pilot was reading, as usual when off
duty; to his question concerning Ken's whereabouts, the

mechanic responded that he was "fooling with his vegetables in the air lock."

"Why does he have to use the lock for a laboratory?" the pilot asked plaintively. "I've already told him it's bad practice. He's got a lab in the station—why doesn't he take them there?"

"I guess he figures if a refrigerator breaks down he can pump the air out of the lock and have a chance of the specimen's lasting until he can make repairs," Feth replied. "I imagine you'd have to ask him, to be really sure. I wouldn't worry—there are just the three of us aboard, and those cases aren't too big to get around if your engines start to get out of hand." The pilot grunted, and returned to his reading; but one eye flickered occasionally to the board of telltale lights. He knew when Ken evacuated the lock and opened the outer door, but apparently did not consider it worth while to ask why. Feth, as a matter of fact, did not know either; he was wondering a good deal harder than Lee. Fortunately the pilot was used to his taciturnity and habitual glumness of expression, or his attitude might have aroused suspicion. It was, as a matter of fact, his awareness of this fact that had caused Ken to refrain from telling his whole plan to Feth. He was afraid the mechanic might look too happy to be natural.

The next interruption caused the pilot to put down his book and rise to his feet. "What's that fool doing now?" he asked aloud. "Drilling holes in the hull?" Feth could understand the source of his worry; the outer door of the air lock had been closed again, and pressure had returned to normal some time before—but now the pressure was dropping rapidly, as though through a serious leak, and air was being pumped *into* the chamber. The outer door was still closed.

"Maybe he's filling some portable tanks," suggested Feth hopefully.

"With what? There isn't a pump on board that could take air faster than the lock bleeders can deliver it, except the main circulators. He's not using those, where he is."

"Why don't you call him and ask, then? I notice the inner door is sealed, too; he'll probably have a fit if you opened it in the middle of his work."

"I'll have one myself if this goes on," growled Lee. He watched the indicators for another moment, noting that the pressure now seemed to be holding steady at about half normal. "Well, if it's a leak, he had sense enough to plug it." He turned to the microphone, switched to the local wavelength used in the suit receivers, and made the suggested call. Ken answered promptly, denying that he had bored any holes in the hull and stating that he would be through shortly. Lee was able to get nothing else from him.

"One would almost think you didn't trust him," gibed Feth as the pilot turned away from the microphone. "You have as much reason to believe him as you have to believe me, and I notice you don't worry much about me."

"Maybe after he's had a few more sniffs I'll feel the same about him," Lee replied. "Right now, just listening to him makes me think he's not convinced yet about being under the influence. I never heard anyone talk like that to Drai before."

"I did—once."

"Yeah. But he's done it more than once. Drai feels the same way—he told me to camp in this control room as long as you two were on board. I don't think it matters, myself—I've got the key, and if anyone can short the whole control system out from under a Bern lock he's darned good. However, orders are orders." He relaxed once more with his book. Feth resumed his gloomy train of thought.

"So they're trusting on just that one hold on us. As if I didn't know it. If Ken could figure out some means of getting at Drai's cold-safe—I certainly have never been able to—but then, we couldn't find Sarr anyway—if only we were looking for a sun like Rigel or Deneb, that a fellow could recognize at thousands of parsecs instead of having to get close enough to spot planets—" his thoughts rolled on, consisting largely of "If only's" as

they had now for years. The drug had won little if anything to Feth's mind, but the fact of his subjection to it
had long since given him an apathetic attitude toward
all suggestions for escape. He wondered why he had
consented to do as Ken asked—how could the scientist
possibly keep the assurance he had given?

Ken's own voice eventually interrupted this line of
cogitation. "Feth, could you come down here to help
me for a moment? I'm nearly through; there's some
stuff I want to take out of the lock." Both Sarrians in
the control room glanced at the indicators. The lock
pressure was rising again.

"All right, I'm coming," replied Feth. "Get the inner
door open as soon as pressure's up." He started down
the corridor, leaving the pilot behind. Ken's message
had been well worded.

He was not gone long enough to make the pilot suspicious; within two or three minutes Lee heard both mechanic and scientist returning. They were not talking,
and as they approached the pilot grew curious. He
started to rise to meet them, but had time just to reach
his feet before the two entered the door. The gloomy
expression had left Feth's face, to be replaced by one
much harder to decipher. Lee, however, spent no time
trying to solve its meaning; his eyes were both drawn
instantly to the object the two were carrying in a cloth
sling between them.

It was roughly cubical, perhaps a foot on a side. It
was yellow in color. It trailed a visible stream of mist,
and yellow droplets appeared and grew on its surface—
droplets of a deeper, honey-colored hue; droplets that
gathered together, ran down the sides of the block,
soaked into the sling, and vanished in thin air. For an
instant Lee, watching it, showed an expression of bewil-
derment; this changed almost at once to one of horror;
then he regained control of himself.

"So that's where the air was going," he remarked.
"What's the idea?"

Ken, who was clad in a space suit except for the helmet, did not answer the question directly. Instead, he asked one of his own.

"You know the coordinates of Sarr, and could get there from here, don't you?"

"Of course. I've made the trip often enough. So what—I hope you don't think I'm going to tell you in order to get out of a frostbite."

"I don't care whether you want to tell us or not. I plan for you to do the piloting. And I don't plan to freeze you on this block—in fact, we'll put it down right here. You have until it evaporates to make up your mind. After that, we'll be in a position to make it up for you." The pilot laughed.

"I was expecting that one. Am I supposed to believe you have some tofacco in the middle of that? You just made the block a couple of minutes ago."

"Quite true. Since you bring up the matter, there *is* a cylinder of tofacco inside the block. I put it there myself—a few minutes ago, as you say."

"I suppose you broke into Laj Drai's safe and borrowed it." The pilot was obviously incredulous.

"No. However, Drai's suggestion of playing on the sympathies of the natives of Planet Three was a very good idea."

"I suppose they gave you a hundred units for rescuing their kids."

"As a matter of fact, it seems to be more like two thousand. I didn't exactly count them, but they're very neatly arranged; and if the unit you mean is one tenth of one of the cylinders they come in, that figure is about right." The pilot might have been just a trifle uneasy.

"But there weren't any landings after Drai had the idea—you couldn't have asked for it."

"Are you trying to insult me by saying I had to wait for Drai to have such an idea? I thought of it myself, but having been brought up with a conscience I decided against trying it. Besides, as I keep saying, I don't know their language well enough yet. As it happened, the native I'd been talking to gave me a container of the stuff without my mentioning it at all. He seems to be a nice

fellow, and apparently knows the value we place on tofacco. I fear I forgot to report that to Drai."

Lee looked positively haggard as the likelihood of the
story began to impress him; Feth, on the other hand,
had brightened up amazingly. Only a slight expression
of doubt still clouded his features—could the scientist
be running a bluff? It seemed impossible; it was hard to
see how getting started for Sarr would do any good unless he had a supply of that drug, and he had made no
mention of forcing Lee to help them get it from Drai's
safe.

These points must have crossed the pilot's mind, too;
he was looking at the dwindling lump of sulfur with a
growing expression of terror. He made one last objection, knowing its weakness even before he spoke.

"You won't dare let it out—Feth has no suit, and you
don't have a helmet."

"What difference does it make to us?"

With that, Lee made a sudden, frantic break for the
door. He dived headlong into Feth, and for a few seconds there was a nightmarish swirling of legs and tentacles. Ken stood by, but his assistance was not needed.
The pilot suddenly rolled back almost to his control
board, tentacles lashing madly; but when he regained
his feet, he did not seem eager to renew the struggle.

"If I'd only had—"

"Yes—it would have been very nice if Drai had let
anyone but himself carry a gun. The fact is, he doesn't;
and you haven't too much time. How about it?" Feth
emphasized his words by turning up the control room
thermostat, which was within his reach.

The pilot gave in. If any shred of doubt about Ken's
truthfulness remained in his mind, he did not dare gam-
ble on it—he had seen drug addicts other than Feth,
and remembered some harrowing details.

"All right—take it away!" he gasped. "I'll do whatever you want!"

Without comment Ken picked up both ends of the
sling and carried the now much lighter bundle back toward the air lock. He was back in two or three minutes.

"Made it!" he said. "I was wondering if it might not boil through before I got there—you held out longer than I thought you would, Lee. However, the air is clear after all. I may mention that that particular block is the top one in my little refrigerator, and it will take remarkably little time to bring it into action.

"Well, let's make plans. I'd rather like to arrest our friend Drai, but I don't quite see how we're to go about it. Any ideas?"

"*Arrest* him?" A faint smile suddenly appeared on Feth's face.

"Yes. I'm afraid I'm some sort of deputy narcotics investigator—not that I asked for the job, and certainly I'm not a very efficient one. Maybe I ought to swear you in, too, Feth—I guess I can do it legally."

"You needn't bother. It was done more than eighteen years ago. Apparently they didn't bother to tell you that the stunt of taking an innocent general science dabbler and trying to make a policeman out of him had been tried before, with no visible results?"

"No, they didn't. I'll have something to say to Rade when we get back. If he knew that—"

"Take it easy on him. Under the circumstances, I'm very glad he tried again. You haven't done such a bad job, you know."

"Maybe not, but the job's not done. I see the reason now for a lot of things that puzzled me about you. As far as I'm concerned, this is your show as much as mine, from now on. How do we go about collecting Drai? I suppose the others aren't worth bothering with."

"Why not leave him where he is? There's no other ship; he's stuck as long as we have this one, unless he wants to take a ride in a torpedo. Since there's nowhere else in this system where he could live for any length of time, I don't think he'll do that. My advice would be to take off right away, and let him worry about what's happened until we get back with official support."

"The motion is carried—except for one thing. I have to run a little errand first. Feth, you keep an eye on our friend and pilot while I'm gone." He disappeared toward the air lock before any questions could be asked.

As a matter of fact, his absence was quite long, and eventually the ship had to go after him. He was in a valley adjacent to that of the station, with a problem he could not handle alone. Sallman Ken liked to pay his debts.

None of the Wings, of course, felt that the strange "fire-man" owed them anything. On the contrary. They did not blame him for the fire—he had been on the ground, talking to them, when the ship started it. The blaze was out by night, anyway, with the aid of the crew from Clark Fork. The only real concern the family felt was whether or not the alien would return.

It was not until evening that anyone remembered that a torpedo load of metal should have arrived that day. Don and Roger went out in the morning to the site of the transmitter, and found a torpedo, but its cargo door was closed and there was no answer to their shouts. This, of course, was the one Drai had sent down, and which he had completely forgotten in the rush of events. It had been operating on radio rather than achronic transmitter control, since the *Karella* had been so near at the time, and there was no way to switch it back from a distance even if the drug-runner's memory should improve. Ken himself, with his "payment" safely on board the *Karella,* never thought of it; his attention had promptly switched to the obvious need for a survey of the Solar System before he left it. A full Earth day had been spent looking briefly over Sol's frozen family, before he could be persuaded to start for home—Feth did not try very hard to persuade him, as a matter of fact, since he had his own share of scientific curiosity. At last, however, they plunged back to make the final call at Planet Three. The transmitter was just emerging into sunlight; this time even Lee appeared willing to home down on it. A mile above the peaks, Ken guided him on a long downward slant to a point above the Wing home.

The natives had seen them coming; all seven of them were standing outside, watching the descent with emotions that Ken could easily guess. He waved Lee into a position that brought the air lock directly over the clearing in front of the house, and the lowest part of the ship's hull thirty feet above the treetops. Then he climbed into his armor, entered the air lock with his "payment," and opened the outer door without bothering to pump back the air. For a moment he was enveloped in a sheet of blue fire, which burst from the port and caused the natives to exclaim in alarm. Fortunately the flame of burning sulfur licked upward, and was gone in a moment. Then Ken, waving the natives away from directly below, rolled his payment over the sill of the lock. It made quite a hole in the ground. A carefully made diagram, drawn on the fluo-silicone material the Sarrians used for paper, followed; and when the Wings looked up after crowding around this, the *Karella* was a dwindling dot in the sky, and Ken was already preparing a report for the planetary ecologists and medical researchers who would return with them. Perhaps a cure for the drug could be found, and even if it weren't he was on good enough terms with the natives so that he needn't worry too much. Not, of course, that that was his only interest in the weird beings; they seemed rather likable, in their own way—

He even remembered to write a brief report for Rade.

On the ground, no one spoke for some time.

"I can't budge it, Dad," were the first words finally uttered. They came from Roger, who had been vainly trying to move the grayish lump that had landed at their feet.

"It must weigh two hundred pounds or so," supplemented Don. "If it's all platinum—"

"Then we'll have a fine time breaking it up into pieces small enough to avoid comment," finished his father. "What interests me right now is this picture." The others crowded around once more.

It was a tiny diagram of the Solar System, such as they had drawn before the fire two days ago. Beside it was the unmistakable picture of a space ship like the *Karella*—heading away from it. Then another diagram, apparently an enlarged view of the orbits of the inner planets, showed the arcs through which each would move in approximately a month; and finally a third picture reproduced the first—except that the space ship was pointing *toward* the system. The meaning was clear enough, and a smile broke out on Mr. Wing's face as he interpreted it.

"I guess we continue to eat," he remarked, "and I guess our friend wants to learn more English. He'll be back, all right. I was afraid for a little while he'd take that carton of cigarettes in the wrong spirit. Well—" he turned to the family suddenly.

"Don—Roger—let's go. If he's going to be away a month, and that torpedo is still lying where you found it, we have a job of tinkering to do. Roger, by the time you're Don's age you may be able to pilot us on a return visit to your hot-blooded friend—we're going to find out how that gadget works!"